THE
COAL-HOLE
MYSTERY

THE
COAL-HOLE
MYSTERY

by Teresa Crompton

CHRISTIAN FOCUS PUBLICATIONS

© 1996 Teresa Crompton
ISBN 1-85792-217-4
reprinted 1999

Published by
Christian Focus Publications Ltd,
Geanies House, Fearn, Ross-shire,
IV20 1TW, Scotland, Great Britain
www.christianfocus.com

Cover design by Donna Macleod
Cover illustration by Geoffrey Edgeler, Allied Artists

Printed and bound in Great Britain by Cox & Wyman
Ltd, Reading, Berks

CONTENTS

Chapter

Chapter One

A New Home

Marilyn Ross shaded her eyes against the cold, bright glare of the February sun in order to see the approaching figure more clearly. Then she gave a sudden little squeak of excitement.

'Aha!' she said to herself. 'Here comes that no good Janet Corby, now I can ask her what she knows about the empty house!'

Marilyn's short, plump form hurried along the village street towards the pond.

'Morning, Janet,' she panted. 'Do you know if anyone's moving into the house next to you, Mrs Coverley's old place?' Finding out other peoples' business was Marilyn's main interest in life and what a good opportunity this was to discover whether the rumours she had heard were true!

Janet Corby, tall with curly brown hair, put down her heavy bag of shopping and smiled her pleasant smile.

She had known Marilyn for years and knew exactly what she was like. She watched as the ducks, hungry in the cold weather, came quacking and splashing across the water. They were hoping for some bread but neither of the women had anything to give them that day.

'Actually I do know something,' Janet replied at last. 'Miss Coverley, the old lady's daughter, was round there on Monday, cleaning the cottage out and doing the garden. She told me that a family from somewhere down south are coming.'

'Southerners!' sniffed Marilyn. 'More of 'em. Here one minute and gone the next. They move in and out of Withamby so quickly that you never even have time to learn their names. What's the use of it, I ask you?'

But Janet went on. 'They've got a little girl, not old enough to go to school, and another one of about ten, your Lisa's age.' Marilyn pulled a face.

'Ugh, don't mention her. Our Lisa gives me nothing but trouble from morning to night; she's a real little horror. Anyway, why do southerners want to live there in that place?' She wrinkled up her nose. 'Old Mrs Coverley didn't exactly spend a lot of money on the house, did she?'

'Well, she was ninety-six when she died, after all,' said Janet. 'And she's been dead and gone six months so it's been empty all winter.' Marilyn shrugged, 'But there's no central heating, and it's riddled with mice, I've heard. I wouldn't live in a place without seeing it first.'

Janet was amused. Everyone in Withamby knew that Marilyn Ross' house was untidy and uncared for and that her two children, Lisa and Tommy, were the same. But she only smiled and said, 'Well, I don't think Miss Coverley wants to sell the cottage yet, after all, it's where she grew up. That's why she's decided to let it out for a while. And she's not got a lot of money to spend on it, either. She knows it's a bit old-fashioned so she's asking very little rent for it.'

'I suppose so,' said Marilyn, grudgingly. Janet picked up her bag and looked down the road.

'Well, I must be getting home. We'll see the new people soon enough, they're due to move in on Saturday. 'Bye, Marilyn,' and she walked on.

*   *   *   *   *

Amy Stewart, aged ten, was bored. The morning had been fun, loading up the car and the big white hired van, saying goodbye forever to their old house and then setting off on the journey. She'd been excited to think about the new house which, her parents had told her, was a little stone cottage in a rural village miles from anywhere. It would certainly be a change from the sprawling suburbs where she'd spent her entire life. But now it seemed as if she'd been sitting in the car for ever.

With all the packing and last minute things to do, the Stewarts had set off much later than planned and had stopped, tired and hungry, for a very late lunch at a fast food restaurant on the motorway. There, Amy had argued with her mother about a strawberry milk-shake and was now in disgrace. Mrs Stewart had said it was

9

too expensive and anyway, it might make Amy sick in the car. Amy had said it wasn't fair and that it was ages since she'd had one.

Now she had no-one to talk to. Her sister, three-year-old Charlotte, was already asleep - full of burger and chips - in her car-seat. Amy looked at the little girl. Even when Charlotte was awake, she thought, she was no fun - too young and too silly.

Mrs Stewart glanced in the mirror. 'He's got stuck behind some big lorries,' she said. Mr Stewart was following the car in a van which was loaded with their household things; toys, books, clothes, and bedding. Mrs Stewart looked in the mirror again, this time at Amy who was pouting.

'Why don't you play a game with the car number-plates?' she asked. 'What about "Anagrams"? Look, that red car has the letters "G" and "DAL" you can make "GLAD," can't you?' Amy looked out of the window at the passing cars with a bored expression on her face.

Mrs Stewart was not happy. The fact that Amy was disobedient and bad-tempered troubled her, but far worse was the sudden change that had come to their lives. Mr and Mrs Stewart hadn't told Amy everything. They didn't want her to know how bad things really were.

Only a few months before life had been going so well. Mr Stewart's job, with a computer company, earned him a lot of money. They'd had a big house in a nice area and had been able to afford to buy lots of things.

But then Mr Stewart had made some mistakes at

work. His boss told him either to leave or take a lower paid job. Mr Stewart didn't want to be unemployed so he took the other job. Now he had to travel about all over the Midlands. He soon realised that he wasn't a very good salesman and he hoped that he would get better in time.

As a result of all this, the Stewarts had to leave their comfortable house in the south and move up to a much smaller, rented one in Lincolnshire.

'The present is bad enough,' thought Mrs Stewart gloomily as she drove along, 'but who knows what the future holds, it might be even worse. It's so humiliating. All this trouble and effort just because of a few mistakes. It's not fair on me or the children,' she grumbled to herself. Her thoughts were disturbed by a voice from the back seat.

'Mum, this game's useless. I can't do it, I can't make any words out of, "NRDF".' Mrs Stewart felt her temper rising and she tried hard to control herself. Amy was causing a lot of trouble today.

'Well play another game then. Try to make a sentence out of them one letter for one word.' She thought for a few seconds and then said, '"NRDF"? How about, "Never Ridicule Daddy's Feet"? That's a good one!'

'What does "ridicule" mean?' asked Amy.

*   *   *   *   *

After half an hour they turned off the motorway onto a small road and soon saw a sign-post saying 'Withamby 4.' They drove on; the sky was overcast and the light already fading. Then, as the car came over the top of a hill Amy saw, for the first time, the village where they were to live. It was laid out before them, the buildings spreading down the slope and out into the valley below. The scene looked cold and dismal.

As the car coasted down the hill the windows of the stone houses stared out at the new arrivals, black and unseeing. Only a few showed lights glowing in the rooms. Mrs Stewart checked in the mirror to see that her husband was still behind.

'Now,' she said. 'Keep your eyes open, Amy. We need to look for "Occupation Lane." I was told that it's down in the valley, on the left. It's such a funny name that we shouldn't miss it.'

They drove slowly through the drowsy village, past a shop with a sign saying, 'Post Office and Stores,' its big glass windows bright in the dusk. They went on, past a duck-pond, until they saw the street-sign they were looking for.

As the car rounded the sharp bend into the narrow lane, Mrs Stewart had to pull up suddenly to avoid an old man who was walking along in the middle of the road. His long black coat was flapping in the breeze and a brown hat was pulled down low over his eyes. He didn't seem bothered by the sudden appearance of the car but stopped dead in his tracks and started to wave his hand about. It was clear that he was saying something but they couldn't hear what it was.

Mrs Stewart steered the car past him carefully. 'One of the local yokels!' she said. 'Now where's our house?

Here we are, Number Six!' and she pulled up outside a dark building on the left side of the road. Little Charlotte woke with a start when they came to a halt and looked around sleepily. 'Are we there?'

'Yes, look, that's our new house,' said Mrs Stewart, trying to sound cheerful as she pointed out of the window. Mr Stewart pulled the van up behind them and the family sat staring out at their new home, each of them with different things going through their minds. Mr Stewart thought how small and old the building was - it would need a lot of work doing on it. Mrs Stewart looked at the old stonework walls, and wondered whether they were damp. Charlotte, meanwhile, was thinking about what was for tea. Amy, gazing up at the little dormer windows set into the low red-tiled roof, wondered which bedroom would be hers.

Number Six, Occupation Lane, Withamby, was a two storey stone cottage, one of a similar pair standing side by side. Between the two was an open gap, a driveway for both. At the top of the driveway the gardens were divided by a high wooden fence. The cottage next door had its downstairs lights on and red curtains drawn - it looked inviting and cosy.

The Stewarts' cottage looked empty and cold. On the front were four windows, two upstairs and two downstairs, but no door - that was round at the back. There was no front garden as the cottages were right on the pavement.

Mrs Stewart steered the car carefully up the driveway and parked it on the lawn at the back, leaving room for her husband to bring the van in. She got out of the car stiffly and Charlotte, suddenly full of energy, ran around happily on the grass.

'Now,' said Mrs Stewart to Amy, 'Miss Coverley said that if she couldn't be here to meet us she'd leave the key under a big stone near the back door.' She started to hunt round.

'It's getting a bit dark but...here we are - a big heavy stone...Ugh!' and she let out a little shriek. She had lifted the stone and, sure enough, the key was there, glinting in the dying light. But so too were some fat shiny earthworms, writhing and rolling helplessly, and wood-lice scuttling in all directions. She picked up the key gingerly and examined it to make sure it didn't have anything nasty sticking to it.

As Mrs Stewart unlocked the cottage door and groped about inside for the light switch, Mr Stewart opned the back door of the van and unloaded the first of the boxes, bags, and cases onto the driveway. The family were all so pre-occupied, that none of them noticed the small, pale face looking down on them from the dark upstairs window of the house next door.

Chapter Two

The House Next Door

In her unlit bedroom Sarah Corby stood silently by the window, looking at her new neighbours. The window was set into the end wall of the house and she could see across the driveway from there and into the dark garden of the cottage next door.

She watched as the two vehicles came up the driveway. First to arrive was the car. Sarah saw a good-looking woman with a short, smart hair-style and two children. One was a girl of about ten wearing leggings and a bright red jumper. Her attractive heart-shaped face was surrounded by wavy brown hair, held back with a red hairband. Her younger sister, a dainty little girl of about three, stretched and yawned in her pink coat. Then a tall, black-haired man pulled up in a white van. The whole family looked tired and stiff, Sarah thought.

Through the thin, dimpled glass of her window, she heard Mrs Stewart's little shriek of horror and saw her and the girls disappear into the house. The man stayed behind outside, unloading things from the back of the van. Soon, he too disappeared inside with a load of bags and boxes. Sarah waited for a couple of minutes but there was nothing else to see, so she went downstairs.

In the warm, low-ceilinged kitchen below, her mother Janet Corby, was standing by the cooker making the evening meal. Sarah's grandfather, jovial Jack Corby, sat by the fire in his old armchair, reading the newspaper. Grandpa worked in the town of Langton, ten miles away, repairing tractors and farm machinery. Years ago he had been a farm-worker and he still had a weather-beaten face and rugged outdoor look about him.

Tabsy, the big tabby-cat, was curled up on the hearth-rug, sharing the warmth of the crackling fire with Grandpa's slippered feet.

'Grandpa,' said Sarah as she shut the door at the bottom of the stairs behind her, 'the new people next door have arrived.' He looked up from behind his paper.

'I thought I heard a car. Have you seen them, love?'

'Yes,' said Sarah, 'there's a girl about my age and a little girl. Their mother was driving the car. A man came behind in a white van.'

'That'll be the Dad, most likely. I wonder what they'll reckon to Number Six, Occupation Lane?' chuckled Grandpa. 'It must be a bit damp in there by now, after being empty all these weeks!' Janet looked thoughtful. 'Tomorrow I'll pop round to see if they need anything, when they've had a chance to get settled in,' she said, curious to see their new neighbours.

Sarah sat down on the hearth-rug and tickled Tabsy's neck; the cat stretched out her front paws and rolled over. Janet glanced at her daughter.

'She's just like I was at that age,' she thought, 'quiet, with short hair and spectacles!' As she was now eleven, Sarah had left the small primary school in the next village the year before to go to the secondary school in Langton. Sarah had something else in common with her mother, too - they were both Christians.

Janet wiped her eyes as she put some chopped onion into the pan. 'Sarah may be like me now,' she thought, 'but I hope she doesn't do all the silly things I did when I was older!'

Janet had left Withamby, where she had grown up, to go to college. But her new freedom went to her head and she started to lead a rather wild life. After a couple of years she had a baby, Sarah. The baby's father didn't want anything to do with his new little daughter. He wasn't interested in Janet any more either - not when she had to give her attention to a baby instead of to him. He soon disappeared and Janet had never seen or heard from him again.

Feeling alone and helpless, Janet had to give up her studies at college to look after Sarah and life had been very hard. Just when it seemed that things couldn't get any worse, they did. Her mother was told she had a serious illness and six months later she died. Janet was desperately unhappy - so desperate that she started to pray to God to help her. He answered her prayers. Soon afterwards she met some Christians who became her friends. They took her to their church and helped her to come to know Jesus.

Then Janet's life got much better. After a while she decided to go back and live at Withamby to look after her father, now that he was on his own. But when she got home she found that she was very unpopular with some of the villagers. Her mother, Mrs Corby, had been well-liked and many people had been shocked when she died so quickly. Some of them had heard stories of the life that Janet had led while she was away and spread rumours, saying to each other:

'It was the worry-it brought on her mother's death!'

Some people knew that Janet was a Christian now, but even that didn't make any difference to those who wanted to think badly of her.

'Just a trick,' they said. 'What a hypocrite pretending she's "holier than thou" after all the trouble she's caused!'

The gossip and rumours upset Janet, especially when they were about her mother. But she carried on living quietly in the village, trying to be friendly with people, and hoping that in time they would see how much Jesus had changed her.

Janet stirred some pieces of carrot into the stew and sighed to herself. 'Poor Sarah, some of the village people don't want their children to have anything to do with her. I hope this new girl next door will be a friend. It would be nice for her to have someone in the village to play with.'

Next door, meanwhile, things were not going well. The house was very cold and the Stewarts had to keep their coats on while they unpacked. Mrs Stewart was trying to make the beds up but not only were the mattresses damp, the pillow cases were lost among all the bags and boxes, too.

'We'll just have to use towels on the pillows instead of pillow cases for tonight,' she said. 'Now where are the hot water bottles?'

One of the three bedrooms was so small that there was only space for a narrow bed in it. There was no room for a wardrobe or even a cupboard. This was to be Charlotte's room.

'She'll just have to share your wardrobe,' Mrs Stewart said to Amy.

'That's not fair - and anyway it's not even big enough for my things, let alone hers as well...' Amy answered back. But Mrs Stewart had had enough of her daughter's bad temper. One look at her mother told Amy not to say any more...for now.

Downstairs, Charlotte was following Mr Stewart around, asking him one question after another about the house. He searched high and low for a new light-bulb for the bathroom but couldn't find one. Next he tried to light a fire in the little living room grate. However, as the house had been empty all winter and the matches and the wood were damp, he couldn't get a fire going at all. Mr Stewart wished he'd been a Boy Scout when he was younger; they were taught how to light fires, he was sure.

With the help of the dry newspaper, Mr Stewart got a fire started at last and the little living room soon felt less chilly and more cheerful. Charlotte was fascinated by the flames and smoke and wanted to play with them. There'd been nothing as exciting as this at their old house! But Mr Stewart quickly put the fire-guard up and explained to her that it was *very* dangerous to play with fire.

Just at that moment, loud squeals came from the kitchen. Mr Stewart and Charlotte ran to the door and found Mrs Stewart and Amy huddled together in a corner.

'A mouse - over there!' shrieked Amy, pointing to the old enamel sink. 'I saw it! It's gone behind the cupboard. You've got to do something, Dad - we can't stay here!'

Chapter Three

The Old Sampler

The grey morning light lit Amy's face softly. Half awake, she rolled onto her side and curled up but it was no use, she wasn't warm enough to sleep. After dozing for a while she sat up and stretched, even though a glance at her watch told her that it was still very early.

The bedroom was small and most of the space was taken up by old furniture. Apart from the bed there was a bedside table, a narrow wardrobe ('which I have to share with Charlotte!' Amy thought crossly), and a huge, heavy dressing table made of dark wood. Down each side of its deep kneehole were four drawers; these were where she would have to keep most of her things because there were no other cupboards in the room.

Amy slipped out of bed, pulled on her warm dressing gown and slippers, and went over to the window. Looking out, she was surprised to discover that her bedroom was at the end of the house. Peering across the driveway she noticed a window facing hers at the end of the next door cottage. But its flowery curtains were shut.

'Someone must be asleep in there,' she thought. 'I wonder who it is?'

Her breath clouded the glass as she looked down into the neighbours' garden. It was neatly kept but there wasn't much lawn to play on, most of the area was dug up for growing flowers or vegetables. Now, a silvery frost greyed the rich dark earth. A few rows of drooping leeks and some Brussel sprout plants could be seen in the soil. Then Amy saw a tabby-cat picking its way delicately over the cold clods of earth; she liked cats.

When the tabby had disappeared from view, Amy tiptoed out onto the landing and peeped round Charlotte's door. The little girl was still sound asleep in her tiny room. Amy was glad, she wanted to explore on her own. Creeping past her parents' bedroom she went downstairs, hoping that the creaking noises of the old wooden floorboards wouldn't wake anyone. At the bottom she unlatched the door which opened directly into the kitchen, and headed across the cold stone flags on the floor for the living room.

Suddenly she froze, then went hot and cold at the same time. She had remembered the mouse! Terrified, she dared herself to glance at the sink where, the night before, they'd seen the small rodent dart off into a hole. But this morning there was no sign of it. Relieved, Amy ran to the living room and went in, closing the door tightly behind her.

As she pulled back the faded chintz curtains, the chilly morning light flooded into the small room. She sat down on the comfortable old sofa and looked round the room, hugging her knees to keep warm. There were only cold, grey ashes in the little fireplace now.

Like that of the rest of the house, the furniture in here was old but solid, 'built to last' as her father had said the night before. The cottage carpets were faded and their patterns old-fashioned but, being made of hardwearing wool, they were still soft and thick.

Amy shivered in the early morning coolness and glanced at the old-fashioned, floral wallpaper. Above the fireplace was a picture showing a landscape with trees and fields and a faraway hill with a castle on top, but it wasn't very interesting. There was only one other picture in the room, a small, dark one in a wooden frame. She got up and went over to look at it.

'What a strange old thing,' thought Amy. She'd never seen anything like it before. The 'picture' was an embroidery. Coloured threads sewn into old linen, mottled and yellowed with age and it looked as if it was a real antique. She peered closer.

Around the edge of the cloth were flowers, delicately embroidered in pink, yellow and green. In the middle there was some writing sewn in tiny stitches. It was in an old style and quite difficult to read but Amy studied it hard. It said:

May Alice Harris
Aged, 12 years
Withamby April 20th 1911

Underneath the writing there was a line of flowers, blue cornflowers and red poppies, the colours faded with age. Then there was some more writing; it looked like a poem:

'As for man, his days are as grass
As a flower of the field, so he flourisheth
For the wind passeth over it
And it is gone. Psa. 103'

Amy was very curious about the picture. Who was May Alice Harris, and what did the strange poem about grass and flowers mean?

Half an hour later, Mrs Stewart came downstairs and found her daughter in the living room sorting through the boxes of toys. As soon as she saw her, Amy said, 'Mum, look at that,' and pointed to the old stitched picture. 'Who's May Alice Harris?'

Mrs Stewart studied the embroidery thoughtfully.

'I didn't notice this last night. It's an old sampler done in cross-stitch. What fine work for a girl of twelve! But then they all learnt to sew well in those days.'

She touched the carving on the dark wooden frame. 'This is done by hand. I'm not sure who the girl is, we'll have to ask someone. It could be that "Harris" was old Mrs Coverley's name before she got married. If that's true it means she must have been brought up in the village - perhaps in this very house. Look, she's sewn "Withamby" here.'

'What's the poem about?' asked Amy.

'Oh, it's not a poem, it's a verse from the Bible, I think. Here it says "P-S-A." That probably means it's from the book of Psalms in the Old Testament. It used to be the fashion to put something from the Bible on these old samplers. Years ago all the girls made one when they'd learnt to sew - it was a way of showing people how good they were with a needle.' She turned away. 'Now, come and help me to find the breakfast things - and keep an eye open for that mouse!'

As there was no milk or butter the children had dry toast with jam, biscuits, and orange squash for breakfast. Charlotte found everything in the new house very exciting. From the uneven stone flags on the kitchen floor to the patches of black mould in the tiny bathroom. It was difficult, for once, to make her stop chattering and eat her food. Mrs Stewart sipped a cup of milkless tea.

'Amy, I'd like you to go up to the village shop - the one we saw yesterday - and buy some things for me. I'll give you a list and the money,' she said.

Amy pulled a face. 'I don't want to go and anyway, I don't know where the shop is.'

'Yes you do,' said Mrs Stewart firmly, her mouth setting hard with irritation. 'You're going! It's easy to get there. You just go to the end of this lane, turn right and walk along till you see it - it's past the duck-pond.'

Outside in the sharp sunshine, Amy found it was a lovely morning, cold and crisp and clear. But she stood on the pavement in front of her new home feeling quite timid, she was out alone in a strange place. But it was exciting, too. 'This must be what it's like to be an explorer,' she said to herself.

Occupation Lane had a strange name but it looked quite ordinary in the bright daylight. Opposite the twin cottages there were two big new houses set back from the road. Each had tall trees in the front gardens and a double garage built on at the side. There weren't many houses in the lane but, looking along to the left, Amy could see in the distance a block of small red-brick cottages on the other side of the road.

As she stared around, Amy didn't notice the strange old man in the ancient black coat walking towards her from the other direction, his head down. She stepped back in surprise as he passed by. The man glanced up at her for a second then trudged on, muttering to himself. Amy thought she heard him say, 'If we'd never 'ave gone, we wouldn't never 'ave 'ad no trouble, we wouldn't.' It didn't seem to make any sense.

In the village shop Amy gave her mother's list to the shopkeeper. While she waited for him to collect the things on it, she looked round. The shop seemed to sell a bit of everything: tinned food and fresh food, socks and shoe polish, toys, sweets, and stationery. Some brown sepia postcards pinned to a board on the wall caught her eye. A sign above them read, 'Edwardian Village Scene Reproductions - 30p.'

Amy studied each of the cards until, with a little shock, she recognised one of the pictures - it was of her new house. The photograph had obviously been taken a long time ago. Standing in the gap between the two houses, in what was now the driveway, there was a tree with wide, low branches.

'That tree's not there any more,' thought Amy and then, looking more closely, she saw that beneath the branches was a girl, dressed in very old-fashioned clothes. The picture wasn't very clear but Amy could tell that the girl had on a long white pinafore over a dark dress, dark stockings, and boots laced up her ankles. Although her light hair was tied back over her forehead, it was so long that it tumbled down her shoulders. The girl was standing stiffly, staring at the camera, perhaps she'd never had her photograph taken before.

Amy wanted a copy of that photo and she wanted it now! The problem was that she didn't have any of her own money with her. In a second she made up her mind to take the 30p from her mother's purse. A few minutes later, she was walking home with the shopping in a carrier bag and the postcard in her pocket, she would study the old picture more closely in private.

Back in Occupation Lane, Amy found her mother in the garden talking to a woman. There was a girl there too with short hair and glasses.

'Amy,' said Mrs Stewart, 'this is Janet Corby and this is Sarah, she's twelve. They live next door so you two girls can be friends, can't you?' Amy stared at Sarah and Sarah smiled back shyly.

'Hello Amy,' said Sarah's mother. 'Why don't you go with Sarah and she can show you our house. It's just the same as yours only the other way round!'

Amy had no choice but to go next door with Sarah.

The two girls went up the narrow stairs to Sarah's bedroom where Tabsy, the tabby-cat, was curled up on the bed. Amy tickled Tabsy under the chin,

'I wish I could have a cat,' she said wistfully.

'Why can't you?' Sarah asked sympathetically.

'My Mum says we can't, she says it's too much trouble,' and Amy got up to look out of the window.

'Oh!' she exclaimed at once, 'that's my bedroom window over there! We both sleep in the end room, opposite each other!'

'We can wave to each other,' said Sarah. Then Amy asked her about the strange old man.

'Oh, that's Albert.' Sarah replied. 'He lives down the lane. He's very old and there's something wrong with him in the head.'

'I think he looks weird...' said Amy, 'weird and creepy, like a big black bat!'

'Oh no, he's alright really. You don't have to be frightened of him. Sometimes he talks to himself and sometimes he won't speak at all, but he won't hurt you. I just say, "Hello" when I see him.'

Soon Amy went home. She wasn't sure whether or not she wanted to be friends with her new neighbour 'Still, if I don't like her I won't have to see much of her because we'll go to different schools and I can keep my curtains shut!'

She thought about her new school. She was to start the following day at the primary school in Colfield which was the next village to Withamby. What would it be like?

28

Chapter Four

The Coal-Hole

In the afternoon Amy helped her parents to unpack. There were lots of things they needed to find among the bags and boxes, including Amy's school kit.

'It's a shame you have to start mid-term,' said her mother, 'I haven't had a chance to buy your new uniform yet but fortunately the school doesn't seem to be very strict about it. We don't want to spend a lot of money on things for that school. You'll only be there for a short time, you'll start at the big one in Langton in September. That's where Sarah Corby, next door, goes.'

Most of the Withamby children went to Colfield Primary School by bus. It picked them up in the village every morning at nine o'clock and brought them back in the afternoon at half-past-three. As Colfield was only two miles away they didn't have a long journey. Mrs Stewart said that on the first day, Monday, she'd take Amy in the car.

Amy liked the school from the start, it was small and friendly and had a happy atmosphere; her only problem was that she didn't have any friends. Her mum told her not to worry. 'You'll make some soon, it just takes a bit of time to get to know people, that's all.'

Amy said she'd like to go on the bus on Tuesday with the other children, so Mrs Stewart and Charlotte walked down with her to the stop near the pond. It was the second stop in the village and some children were already on board when the bus arrived promptly at nine o'clock. Amy got on and looked up the aisle at the faces. She didn't want to sit alone but most of the children were already sitting in pairs.

Then she saw a face she recognised - a girl from her class. The girl was sitting on her own and so Amy sat down beside her. The bus pulled off and Amy waved goodbye to her mother and Charlotte, then turned to look at her companion. The girl was fiddling with a ragged piece of red ribbon which was tied limply to the end of her long plait of brown hair. She stared back at Amy with a look of curiosity on her plump face and asked,

'You're the new girl who lives in Mrs Coverley's old house, aren't you?' Amy was surprised.

'Yes, how do you know?'

'My Mum told me. What's your name? Mine's Lisa, Lisa Ross,' said the girl. 'I live up that end of the village,' and she jerked her thumb backwards. 'Everyone in Withamby knows my Mum - she's called Marilyn. I've got a brother called Tommy. I hate him, he's a little pig.'

She paused, pulling angrily at her hair-ribbon, then went on. 'You live next door to Sarah Corby, don't you? She's a real idiot - always hanging round with her Mummy.' And Lisa screwed up her face and made a noise like a crying baby. Amy giggled. Then, out of the bus window, she saw the old man, Albert. He wasn't wearing his brown hat and Amy could see that he was nearly bald.

'Oh, look!' she said, 'I saw him when we arrived.' Lisa laughed. 'You'll see him a lot - he's always walking round. Everyone knows old Albert.' She laughed and then started to mumble, making fun of him. Amy thought it was very funny, even if it was a rude thing to do.

'And his sister's nearly as bad,' continued Lisa. 'They live together in a house down your road. She shouted at me once. I call her "Batty Nelly" but she should be called "Batty Hattie" with the things she wears on her head! My Mum says she must have got them out of the Ark!' Lisa stuck out her bottom lip, 'She doesn't like me.'

'Why not?'

'Oh, I nicked some flowers out of her garden once,' said Lisa, carelessly. 'I don't care. Batty Nelly doesn't bother me, I'll get back at her one day.' She looked mischievously at Amy, her eyes dancing. 'If I tell you a secret, will you promise not to tell?' Amy agreed eagerly.

'Well,' said Lisa, whispering, 'Albert's got something secret hidden in their coal-hole. I don't know what it is but I'm going to find out!'

Amy was intrigued. 'What's a "coal-hole?"'

Lisa laughed, rather nastily. 'You don't know much, do you?' she said and then spoke as if Amy was a little child. 'A coal-hole is a very small shed where they used to put coal in the old days, but now most people have central heating so they use them for other things or some people just knock them down. I tell you what,' she went on, speaking normally now, 'I'll come round to your house on Saturday and then we can go out and I'll show you, OK?'

Amy agreed rather uneasily. For some reason she felt nervous about introducing her new friend to her parents. She wasn't sure they'd like Lisa Ross.

*   *   *   *   *

Amy's first week at the new school went well. Lisa moved tables to sit with her and Amy was pleased - it was nice to have an instant friend. True, Lisa was bossy and not many of the other children seemed to like her much. She was always boasting to Amy about all the bad things she'd done.

To try to look just as clever and brave as her new friend Amy told Lisa about stealing from Mrs Stewart's purse to buy the photo from the shop, and then said that she often took money. This wasn't really true; in fact she had only ever done it once before in her life. But try as she might, Amy couldn't compete with Lisa's stories of cutting off all Tommy's hair when he was little, or opening a field gate to let a flock of sheep run all over the village.

Friday came quickly and on the school bus on the way back to Withamby Lisa said, 'I'll see you tomorrow. We go shopping in Langton in the morning but I'll come round after lunch and then...' she started to whisper, '...I'll show you the coal-hole!'

Amy got home to find her mother and Charlotte in the kitchen.

'Good news,' said Mrs Stewart as soon as Amy came in, 'we've caught a mouse!' Mr Stewart had set several traps; he thought there were at least two mice living in their kitchen, and maybe more.

'Ugh!' said Amy. 'Where is it?'

'It's under there!' shouted Charlotte excitedly, pointing to the cupboard under the sink, 'It's got a long tail!'

'I don't dare touch it,' shivered Mrs Stewart. 'Dad doesn't get in till late tonight but I'll leave it for him to deal with, all the same.' Seeing Amy's face she said, 'I know mouse-traps are horrible, but it's better than having dirty little animals nibbling your food before you do, isn't it?'

Amy went upstairs to change. She had some homework and decided to do it now, rather than leaving it over the weekend. By the time she'd finished it was tea-time. She sat with Charlotte at the old wooden kitchen table. Suddenly Mrs Stewart said, 'Oh, I've been meaning to ask you, Amy, where did you get that old photograph I saw in your bedroom?'

Amy went red. She hadn't wanted her mother to find the picture because she'd stolen the money to buy it.

'From the village shop,' she said quietly, taking a big bite of bread.

'It's a lovely photo,' said Mrs Stewart, not noticing Amy's discomfort. 'I'm sure that girl standing outside this house must be Mrs Coverley when she was young. How funny that there used to be a tree between these two cottages. I wonder what happened to it?'

Amy forgot about the stolen money, 'Do you really think the girl is Mrs Coverley?' she asked excitedly. 'That means the photo was taken when she was May Alice Harris, doesn't it?'

'Yes,' said her mother, 'but she looks younger than twelve in the photo; I think she's perhaps only nine or ten, maybe your age.'

Amy looked round the kitchen. How strange to think that eighty years ago May Harris, the girl who had stitched the old sampler, had sat here in her black laced boots, her long fair hair falling over a white pinafore. Had she been scared of the mice, Amy wondered?

After lunch on Saturday, Lisa arrived. Amy introduced her to her parents and then the two girls went upstairs. As the door onto the stairs closed behind them Mrs Stewart wondered why they looked so secretive.

'I don't like the look of Amy's new friend,' she thought. 'She's got a shifty look in her eye.'

In the bedroom, Lisa sat on the bed and looked around.

'You've got a nice room,' she said wistfully. Amy was surprised, she didn't think it was particularly nice, being so small and crowded.

'Tommy's always coming into mine and messing my things up and breaking them and scribbling on my wallpaper,' Lisa went on. 'Doesn't your sister mess your room up?'

'No,' said Amy. 'My Mum wouldn't let her.'

Then Lisa explained her coal-hole plan. They would tell Mr and Mrs Stewart that they were going out for a walk down Occupation Lane, which was true. Then they would go to the terrace of little red-brick houses - Albert and Nelly's house was on the end of the block.

'We just go up the drive at the side and round the back,' said Lisa. 'You keep a look-out while I check out the coal-hole.'

'But what if someone sees us?' asked Amy, troubled.

'Oh, we can just make something up, you can say you've lost your cat.'

'But I haven't got a cat.' Lisa looked at Amy with a tired expression on her face, 'Well, say something else then!'

It was just a short walk along the road.

'That's Albert and Nelly's house with the brown door,' said Lisa. 'The coal-hole's round the back.' She glanced up and down the empty lane.

'Come on,' she muttered. The two girls walked up the concrete drive beside the block of cottages. Albert and Nelly's garden was on their left, a patch of grass with neat borders round the edge. There were already clumps of white snowdrops growing and some new shoots coming up through the dark soil. It was clear that Nelly loved flowers, it was no wonder she'd got cross when Lisa picked them!

Lisa nudged Amy and nodded towards a very small brick shed with a faded blue door, a lean-to built onto the back of the house.

'That's the coal-hole!' she whispered. 'Now you check there's no-one in the kitchen and then I'll try that door.'

Amy's heart started to thump - she couldn't move. Lisa pushed her and hissed urgently, 'Quick!'

Amy went forward and peeped over the kitchen windowsill - the room was empty. She shook her head at Lisa who was standing out of sight of the window and the girl ran quickly and crouched by the blue door. Grasping the round brown knob she turned it and pulled...nothing happened. She turned it the other way...still nothing happened. Amy stood frozen, what if someone saw them? At last Lisa ran back.

'Locked!' she said crossly. 'Come on, let's go.'

As the two girls walked quickly off down the lane Lisa looked thoughtful.

'We'll have to try something else,' she said, half to herself and half to Amy. 'What's old Albert got in his coal-hole that's so important that he keeps it locked up, anyway?'

Chapter Five

Old Albert

February blew itself into March, and March into a wet and windy April. Then the evenings grew lighter and spring was definitely on its way. The Stewarts were settling down to life in Withamby. They liked the peace and quiet and the clean air of the countryside. Charlotte had started at the Village Hall playgroup and Mrs Stewart was getting to know some of the other mothers.

The family were happy in their new house. Mrs Stewart worked hard to make the little cottage into a home without spending much money. She had re-arranged the heavy wooden furniture and shortened curtains which she had brought from their old house. Bright cushions had been scattered on the sofa and chairs in the living room.

Mrs Stewart tried not to remember the large four-bedroomed house they'd left behind, with its spacious conservatory, useful utility room, and two big warm bathrooms.

As for Mr Stewart, he had become an expert at lighting the fire in the living room. 'It's a science,' he explained to his family, and was glad when the house lost its musty, empty smell.

Outside in the garden the grass was growing again after its winter rest. Everyone was pleased to see daffodil and narcissus blooms, as well as shoots of other flowers crowding up through the soil in the borders. Mr Stewart did some gardening and began to think about building a shelter at the side of the house for the car - if he could find the time or the energy. Although he worked very hard and travelled so much that sometimes he had to spend nights away from home, he didn't seem to be able to earn any more money, however hard he tried.

As the weeks and then months passed, Amy and Charlotte's nice clothes got older and shabbier and they started to grow out of them. 'Mum,' said Amy one day, 'my red dress is too short now and my black trousers have got a hole in them. Can I have some new ones?' She'd always had lots of smart clothes in the past so her mother's reply surprised her.

'Next time I go to Langton I'll have a look in the charity shops for you - or there's that good cheap stall on the market on Saturdays.'

Amy and Lisa were best friends now. They went on walks together around the village and soon Amy knew the fields, paths, and tracks of Withamby almost as well as Lisa did. They often saw Albert. He seemed to spend a great deal of his time just wandering around. Sometimes the girls followed the old man, pretending they were spies and he was a suspicious character. They hid behind trees and hedges, watching him.

But Albert was not a very interesting suspect. He never noticed the girls as he walked along with his head down. Sometimes he talked to himself. The only time he looked up was when he passed someone; then he raised his head to give them a glance. If he knew them he gave a swift salute; if he didn't he looked down again. In fact, as the girls discovered, Albert was only ever really sociable when it came to horses.

There were several in the village's paddocks and fields; most were ponies kept for children to ride but some were proper big horses. Albert knew them all and they knew him, too. When they saw him approaching they ambled over to the gates of their fields because Albert always had something for them in the deep pockets of his old black coat. Then he stroked their soft muzzles, patted their arched necks, and mumbled into their ears.

'They're probably the only ones who can understand what he's saying,' Lisa said.

One Sunday afternoon the two girls were out on a walk when they saw Albert in the distance.

'Let's follow him,' said Amy, and the pair darted behind a wall and peeped out over the top just in time to see Albert turn down Brook Lane.

'Come on,' said Lisa and they ran along to keep up with the old man. They followed him until he had passed the last house on the edge of the village. Then, all of a sudden he stopped in his tracks and stood as still as a statue in the lane, peering into a copse which was all overgrown with trees, bushes, and brambles.

'What's he doing?' Amy asked.

'He's thinking about when he used to live there,' said Lisa. What did she mean? Amy couldn't see a house, just a piece of waste land. 'Don't you know?' Lisa said scornfully, 'His family had a house there, years ago when he and Nelly were kids.'

'What happened to it, then?'

'It burnt down. Their Dad was killed in the fire it was too hot for anyone to go in and save him. Before that they were quite rich, I heard. But after the fire they had nothing left and nowhere to live so they moved into that little place near you. I heard that the owner of it took pity on them and let them have it for free, without paying any rent. Bit of a dump, I think.'

Amy looked along the lane just in time to see the old man disappearing into the copse. For the first time she felt sorry for Albert. She could almost see him as a boy, standing there watching his house burning down and knowing that his father was still inside. She didn't tell Lisa how she felt; she knew her friend would only laugh at her. Lisa never seemed to feel sorry for anyone except herself.

'Was it the fire that made him go strange in the head?' asked Amy.

'I don't know,' Lisa replied. 'Some people say he was weird before.' Suddenly she whispered, 'Look, he's coming back, he didn't stay in there long! Let's hide here until he's gone past.'

Albert came trudging heavily back up the lane, his head seeming to hang lower than usual. He didn't notice the girls crouching behind the gate, but as he passed by Amy heard him mutter, 'May 'Arris, May 'Arris. That were what did it, that were!' Amy could hardly believe her ears. What had the girl on her old photo got to do with Albert? Amy didn't want to say anything about it to Lisa - this was a secret she wanted to keep all to herself.

That evening she was sitting in the living room alone. She felt sad but she didn't know why. Restlessly she got up from the sofa and went over to the old sampler on the wall. She looked at the flowers and trees and then she studied the Bible verse carefully. It was the first time that she'd tried to understand what it meant.

'*As for man, his days are as grass,*' she read out loud, '*As a flower of the field, so he flourisheth, For the wind passeth over it, And it is gone.*'

It was very mysterious and the language was so old-fashioned.

As she stood puzzling over it her mother came in.

'Mum, what does it mean?' Amy asked. Mrs Stewart read the stitched words thoughtfully. At length she said, 'I think it means that peoples' lives are like the flowers and grass in the fields. They grow, blossom - then they get old and die.' She smiled wryly. 'It happens to all of us, in time!' Then she picked up her apron which was lying on a chair and went back to the kitchen.

Amy sat for a while looking at the sampler. She thought about twelve-year-old May Harris sitting in this very room all those years ago, her fair head bent over her work as she stitched away carefully at the sampler. Then she remembered old Mrs Coverley who had lived alone in the house until she got so old that she died. And yet the young girl and the old lady were the same person. Only time separated them.

Amy remembered the photograph in her bedroom and went upstairs to fetch it. She knew she'd put it in top drawer of the dressing table, where she kept her paper and crayons and felt-tip pens, but it was very untidy. She scrabbled about. Where was that photo? Had it got caught at the back? Amy reached her hand far into the deep drawer and felt a piece of card, it must be her picture. She pulled it out and stared in surprise. It wasn't her photo but another one altogether!

This one was very old. It wasn't just a reproduction like the postcard she'd bought in the shop, but a genuine old photograph. It showed a man and a woman on their wedding day, standing side by side in front of some trees. The photograph was in black and white. The man had a moustache and was wearing a dark suit with baggy trousers. The lady had on a white dress which came down nearly to her ankles. On her feet were white shoes with pointed toes and on her head a broad-brimmed hat. She was holding a posy of flowers and smiling. The man was smiling too; they both looked very happy.

Amy turned the photograph over. On the back was some writing; it was in pencil and very faint. Curiously she held it up to the bedside light and read: '*June 30th, 1927. Withamby.*'

'That must be the date of the wedding,' Amy mused, 'but who are they?' She looked again at the happy couple. 'It's been there for years and years. Miss Coverley must have missed it when she cleared out her mother's things.' Then a thought struck her. She laid the old photo down carefully on the dressing-table, pulled the drawer right out, and emptied the things onto the carpet. Searching through them she found her photo, the one showing the girl under the tree, between the pages of a sketch book. Holding both pictures side by side she studied them in turn.

'I can't see whether her hair is fair because it's tied up under that big hat,' she thought as she peered closely at the happy face of the smiling bride, 'but I wonder if it's the same person?'

Chapter Six

'Batty Nelly'

It was the middle of June - almost midsummer - and in the Withamby fields the crops were just beginning to turn from green to gold. Haytime was almost here. White Clover, Timothy Grass and Rye Grass swayed softly in the summer breezes. As soon as they came into flower and the seeds began to form the sharp knives of the farmers' grass mowers would cut them down. The hay would make good, sweet winter food for the farm animals.

One bright morning the sun was streaming in through the living room windows of Number Eight, Occupation Lane. Tabsy was asleep on the sofa, her fur soaking up the warm sunshine, while Mrs Stewart and Janet, good friends now, chatted over their cups of coffee. Despite the lovely weather, Mrs Stewart was not happy.

'Have you got mice in your kitchen?' she asked Janet. Her friend laughed,

'No! But we would have if it weren't for Tabsy. Grandpa says she's the best mouser he's ever seen,' and she leaned down to stroke the sleeping cat.

'Well, *we* have. We've set traps and caught a few. I'm hoping we can get rid of them completely.' Janet was sympathetic but doubtful.

'The trouble with these houses,' she said, 'is that the mice seem to keep getting in, whatever you do.' Mrs Stewart groaned,

'But I can't live with mice in the house - they're such dirty little things!'

'Why don't you get a cat?' Mrs Stewart pulled a face, 'I don't want one - please don't suggest it to Amy and Charlotte or I'll never hear the end of it. I know they'd love to have one!'

'Would you like another cup of coffee?' Janet asked as she got up to open the window. 'It's rather stuffy in here, isn't it...what a lovely day...mmm...' and she took a deep breath of the fresh air.

While Janet was in the kitchen, Mrs Stewart sat glumly in the armchair. She was feeling very sorry for herself and had come round in order to have, 'a good moan,' as she called it.

'It's alright for her,' she said to herself. 'There aren't any unwanted visitors in her kitchen. And she hasn't got a husband like mine whose job doesn't pay enough to keep us all fed and clothed properly.' Then a thought struck Mrs Stewart and she realised she was being unkind - Janet didn't have a husband at all!

When Janet came back with the coffee Mrs Stewart

asked, 'How did you cope when Sarah's Dad ran off?'

'Well, it wasn't easy, I admit,' said Janet. 'I didn't know anything about babies and Sarah had colic and cried for half the night. I was so exhausted and lonely.'

'And then your Mum died, didn't she?'

'Yes, it was dreadful. We kept hoping that the treatment would work but instead she just got worse and worse.'

Mrs Stewart discovered that thinking about someone else's problems made hers seem much less important.

Then Janet said something which surprised her.

'But some good came out of the suffering. You see, because of it all I became a Christian.'

'Oh!' Mrs Stewart was embarrassed. She didn't know what to say but Janet went on. 'After that I felt better about Richard, that was Sarah's Dad's name, I could forgive him for deserting me and I could accept my Mum's death, too.' She looked at her friend. 'I realised just how wrong I'd been, following my own way had led me into doing some very silly things. Instead of making me happy it brought me nothing but trouble.

'Then some Christian friends explained that if I told Jesus about my sins, all the wrong things I'd ever done, He would take them away and make my heart clean, if that was what I really wanted.' Mrs Stewart felt uncomfortable and looked at the carpet, blushing. She hoped her friend didn't notice.

'How clean is my heart?' she wondered for a moment.

Janet continued, 'I found it was much better to do what God told me instead of doing what I wanted to do.

I could even be glad that the bad things had happened, because they made me call out to Jesus for help.'

Mrs Stewart was listening carefully. She found it very strange that Janet should be glad about bad things happening, 'I don't believe I ever could be!' she said to herself, thinking again about her own problems. Then she sighed, wishing that she had Janet's faith and trust in Jesus.

Upstairs in her bedroom Sarah was standing by the window, looking down into the Stewart's garden below. She could see Mr Stewart, digging the border with a garden fork, Amy on the lawn making a daisy chain, and Charlotte playing happily on her yellow tricycle in the bright sunshine.

Sarah watched the girls and wished that she had a sister.

Sarah sat down on her bed. 'Lord Jesus,' she said, 'I pray for them and for Mrs Stewart. Please make them all want to know you, so that they can become Christians. Amen.' She often prayed for the Stewarts, especially Amy. She had tried to be friends with her but Amy was always with Lisa Ross. Sarah knew that Lisa didn't like her and suspected, quite rightly, that she had turned Amy against her.

Suddenly Sarah's thoughts were disturbed by a yell from the garden next door. She jumped up to look out of the window again and saw Mr Stewart hobbling painfully towards his house with Amy and Charlotte beside him. They were looking very worried and Charlotte was crying. Then Amy came running round the end of the fence into the Corbys' garden. Sarah hurried downstairs where she found Amy already in the kitchen, saying to Mrs Stewart,

'Mum, Dad's hurt his foot he says can you come quickly?' Mrs Stewart looked worried.

'Sorry Janet, but I'd better go. I'll see you later,' and she and Amy hurried away.

But only five minutes later they were back.

'He's stuck that garden fork through his Wellington boot and skewered his foot,' explained Mrs Stewart. 'I don't know how he did it but it's a very dirty wound and we think he should have a tetanus injection and get it cleaned up.'

Janet was concerned, 'Is there anything I can do to help?'

'Well, we're going to the Langton hospital. We'll have to take Charlotte with us but do you think you could look after Amy until we get back? I'd be very grateful.'

Janet said she'd be glad to, and that Amy could have lunch with them if need be. Mrs Stewart hurried away and Amy was left standing in the Corby's kitchen, staring at Sarah and Janet. She didn't want to stay with them at all.

But they soon made her feel very welcome with orange juice and biscuits and kind questions about her father's accident. After a while Janet said, 'I've got an idea. I don't think your Mum and Dad will be back for at least an hour and a half, Amy, so it would be a good thing for Sarah to take you round to see Miss Collins.' She looked at her daughter,

48

'Grandpa has a glut of lettuce and radishes in the garden at the moment so we can give some to her - I know she likes salad.'

Carrying the vegetables in a bag, the two girls set off down Occupation Lane.

'Who's Miss Collins?' Amy asked.

'Oh, it's Nelly - you know, Albert's sister.' Amy was secretly horrified. Going to see Batty Nelly! How could she get out of it? But she knew she couldn't, so she tried to cheer herself up. Nelly might not be that bad after all, she told herself, Lisa was wrong about some things.

Sarah knocked at the brown door and Amy fidgetted nervously as they waited for someone to answer. Then a thought struck her, what if it was Albert who came to the door? But the next moment a very small old lady appeared. Although it was a warm day she was wearing a bright yellow woollen headscarf, tied under her chin, but apart from that she didn't look too batty.

'Hello, dear,' said Nelly cheerfully, smiling at Sarah with obvious pleasure, 'come on in. Who's your friend?' The two girls stepped into the narrow hallway.

'This is Amy, she's moved in next door,' said Sarah. They all went through into the living room. Amy looked round to see whether Albert was there and felt very relieved when he wasn't. She was surprised to find that everything was so bright and spick and span. Nelly invited them to sit down.

'So you've moved into Mrs Coverley's house, then?' she asked Amy. 'She was a lovely person, I was sad when she passed away. She was ninety-six but she didn't look a day over ninety!'

They sat down. The old lady took the lid off a small tin and offered it round to the girls.

'Mint humbugs,' she said, 'Albert's favourite!' The girls took one each.

'Yes...Mrs Coverley,' Nelly went on. 'It was her heart that gave out in the end.' Then her face clouded over for a moment, 'Poor Albert, his heart's not so good either. The doctor gave him some tablets but he won't take them. He says he's never had a day's illness in his life and he isn't going to start taking 'doctors' quackery' at his age. He's that stubborn, is Albert!' And she giggled, 'I would miss him if anything happened to him. He's eighty now,' she sighed, 'and he's so helpful around the house. He does all the vacuuming, you know, and the washing-up.'

Amy was surprised. She hadn't thought of the old man as doing anything at all except walking round the village. It was odd, too, that his sister seemed so normal. Amy actually liked 'Batty Nelly.'

She was interested in what the old lady had said about Mrs Coverley and asked timidly, 'Miss Collins, did Mr Coverley have a moustache?'

Nelly was surprised. 'Well yes dear, he did when he was younger. Quite a handsome man, as I recall. Of course, they were both older than we were.'

'When did they get married?' asked Amy.

'Oh,' said Nelly, 'now let me think.' And she put her head on one side thoughtfully. Then her face fell, 'It was

1927, of course. In June. Why did it take me so long to remember? The wedding was up in the village church there. A bad year for us, that was, a bad year with everything that happened.' She sunk down into her chair, lost in her own thoughts. She looked so sad that Amy wished she hadn't asked so many questions.

There was a long silence, then Sarah said, 'Grandpa sent you some radishes and lettuce out of the garden,' and she held up the knobbly plastic bag. The old lady brightened immediately.

'Oh, how kind of Jack,' she said. 'Please thank him very much, he is good to me. I do wish Albert would dig up the back garden and grow some vegetables but he's not interested. The only things he cares about are the horses and sorting out his coal-hole!' Nelly rocked back in her chair and laughed.

'Sorting out his coal-hole,' repeated Amy to herself. 'I must tell Lisa that! And what does Batty Nelly find so funny about it?'

* * * * *

As soon as the two girls had left the house Janet started the washing up. As she worked she thought about Mrs Stewart. 'She did seem interested when I told her about Jesus,' she said to herself. 'I'll watch and wait for the right time to tell her more about Him.'

But just then something happened which took Janet's mind off her friend - and everything else, for that matter.

It started when she heard the postman come round the corner of the house, whistling. He pushed some letters through the letter box and they fell onto the doormat with a 'plop.'

Janet dried her hands and went to pick them up. There were five; three were for her father and two for herself. One of hers was only a circular but the other looked more interesting, it was a personal letter. She studied the envelope curiously.

'Strange!' she thought. 'I'm surprised it got here with that address on.' For on the front of the envelope was written only:

Janet Corby
Withamby
Lincolnshire

Who could it be from? Janet looked at the postmark - *'Nottingham.'* She was none the wiser, she didn't know anyone who lived there.

'Only one way to find out,' she thought, tearing open the blue envelope and pulling out the folded sheets of writing paper.

But what Janet read made her go white, then red, and reach for a chair. She sat still for a long time, deep in thought, holding the letter with a limp hand. Her mind was busy but her eyes were blank as she stared out of the window and up into the clear blue sky. After a while she came to herself, stuffed the letter deep into her pocket, and carried on with the washing up.

Chapter Seven

The Riding Lesson

Mr Stewart had to stay at home for a whole week, and all he could do was hobble around the house with a bandage on his foot. Mrs Stewart was worried; every day that he had off work was another day on which he'd earn no money.

Amy, meanwhile, was impatient to tell Lisa her news. Monday morning came at last and at nine o'clock she climbed onto the school bus and sat down beside her friend. Lisa, who was sitting with her arms folded, didn't look up or say 'hello,' but Amy was so eager that she didn't notice.

'Guess what I did on Saturday?' she asked at once, trying to sound mysterious. But Lisa was obviously in a bad mood. 'Can't imagine,' she said shortly.

'I went to Batty Nelly's house!'

'Oh really,' Lisa's tone was sarcastic. 'So I suppose you two are best mates now.' Amy went red

'Nelly's not that bad, honestly. She's not really batty, not when you get to know her. I thought you'd be interested, that's all.'

Lisa didn't reply. She looked out of the window for a while but in the end her curiosity got the better of her and she burst out suddenly, 'So why did you go round there, anyway?'

'I had to,' said Amy, pleased that Lisa was interested at last. 'My Dad hurt his foot and went to hospital and I had to stay with Sarah Corby.'

'Sarah Corby!' sneered Lisa. 'You're a little traitor. I suppose you'll be going round with her and her precious Mummy now, won't you?'

Amy didn't know what to say and so she didn't say anything. The two girls sat in silence for a while until Lisa began again, 'Well, come on then, tell me what happened at Batty Nelly's with sicky Sarah.'

Then Amy told her all about the visit, and everything the old lady had said about Albert and the coal-hole. Lisa was so interested that she forgot her bad mood, 'What did she mean, "sorting out"?' she pondered. 'What's Albert got in there that needs "sorting out"?'

'It can't be things for the garden,' said Amy, 'because Nelly said he's not interested in gardening.'

'I've just got to get inside that shed and find out, but I don't know how!' Lisa grumbled.

*   *   *   *   *

Coming home on the bus Lisa said, 'I'm going riding tonight, do you want to come?' Amy was surprised.

'What, you mean you're having a riding lesson?' But Lisa laughed at her, 'Don't be silly I couldn't afford that! No, I'm going riding a horse, like I said. I'll come round for you at four o'clock.' She wouldn't say anything more about it until, at quarter-past-four, the two girls were going up the hill towards the edge of the village.

It was a lovely afternoon. The sun was shining brightly and above their heads cumulus clouds mounted up, white and puffy and magnificent, into the blue sky. Fields stretched away into the distance. In some of them the wheat, barley, and oilseed grew tall and strong; they were ripening fast now, turning gold and pale. In other fields, sheep or horses grazed contentedly whilst above them larks soared and twittered in the clear sky.

The weather had been perfect for haymaking that week and the farmers had wasted no time. Now neat rows of cut grass striped several meadows. The new mown green hay needed to lie in the fields, drying out in the sun, before it could be baled up and carted away to be stored in barns until the winter when it would provide food for the livestock. Amy watched across the valley as a tractor, tiny in the distance, pulled a tedder up and down between the rows. The tedder fluffed up the hay, allowing the warm air and sunshine to dry it out more quickly.

Her happy mood vanished suddenly when Lisa stopped at the gate of the field of the biggest horse in Withamby. It was a chestnut, with a white diamond on its forehead, and a long and glossy mane and tail. It belonged to Mr Jenkins who bred race-horses and this one did look very well-bred, with a high back, a tall curved neck.

Amy had always felt a little frightened of this horse, it was such a big, awe-inspiring, creature.

Lisa took out some grubby sugar lumps from her pocket. 'Right,' she said to Amy. 'When it comes over here, you attract its attention with these while I stand on the gate and get on its back.'

Amy was amazed and shrank back in horror, 'You can't do that!'

'Why not?'

'Because the horse...it...it's huge - it might hurt you and anyway, you can't ride it without a saddle.'

Lisa looked down her nose. 'It's only a horse,' she said decidedly. 'I've seen people on Westerns on the television riding bareback,' and she started to whistle to the big animal. It was clear that her mind was made up.

The girls whistled, called, clapped, held out the sugar lumps and even handfuls of grass, but it was no good. The horse watched them suspiciously, snuffing the air, and stayed where it was in the middle of the field.

'Come on, let's go and get it,' said Lisa at last, climbing onto the gate.

'I'm not going into the field with it,' said Amy, who didn't like this game at all.

Lisa, ignoring her, got over the gate and strutted off towards the middle of the field without another word. Amy stayed where she was, watching her friend striding towards the tall horse. As Lisa got nearer she slowed down, going forwards one step at a time, holding out the sugar lumps. Soon the horse was eating them out of her hand. Amy noticed how tiny Lisa looked beside the big animal.

Then Amy saw her reach up, quick as a flash, to grab the horse's mane, she was trying to climb up onto its back! But the animal was nearly as quick and when it felt Lisa's hand it pulled away sharply. Amy saw the horse swing round and kick out at her friend with its back legs, catching her on the shoulder with a sharp hoof.

Then, two things happened at once. Lisa let out a yell and fell to the ground. At the same moment, Amy heard someone, somewhere, start to shout.

Amy scrambled quickly over the gate and started running across the grass to where Lisa lay. She was glad to see the horse prance off to a far corner of the field.

Lisa lay motionless in the grass. Amy knelt down beside her and touched her gently on the shoulder,

'Lisa,' she said urgently. 'Are you alright?' Lisa opened one eye.

'Don't touch me there idiot!' she said crossly. 'That's where that brute kicked me.' Amy breathed a sigh of relief; she could tell that Lisa's pride was hurt more than her shoulder!

Then she heard the shouting again - it was coming from behind her. She looked round and saw Albert, standing by the gate, waving his arms in the air and bellowing at them across the paddock. The girls couldn't hear what he was saying but it was plain that he was very angry. Lisa struggled to get up, wincing with pain.

'Quick!' she said, pointing with her good arm to a section of fencing in the hedge on the opposite side of the field from Albert, 'Let's go over there, hopefully he won't have recognised us.'

The girls set off, stumbling over the rough grass, Lisa cradling her throbbing arm as she ran. At the fence they looked back - first at the horse which was now quietly eating as if nothing had happened, and then at Albert who was still standing by the fence, glaring across at them.

'I've never seen him so excited,' said Lisa. 'What's his problem?'

*   *   *   *   *

Lisa's shoulder wasn't broken, just badly bruised. Back at home when Marilyn, her mother, asked her what had happened, Lisa told a lie and said she'd fallen off a gate. As for Amy, she didn't tell her parents about the horse-riding adventure. She had a feeling they'd be very cross with her. She was beginning to forget about the whole episode when on Friday evening, just as the Stewarts were starting their meal, there came a knock at the door.

As Mr Stewart opened the door Amy turned to see who the visitor was. A policeman and a policewoman stood in the doorway. At first Amy was surprised, why should they come? But then she remembered the horse and began to feel very frightened. Mr Stewart invited the police into the living room and sure enough, after a short while he called Amy through. By this time she was nearly crying and Mrs Stewart was very worried too.

'Amy,' said the policewoman, 'were you trying to ride Mr Jenkins' horse on Wednesday?'

'No,' replied Amy miserably. The policewoman watched her, kindly but firmly. 'Do you know who was trying to ride the horse then?' Amy was silent for a moment and then she broke down. The policeman and policewoman looked at each other. They asked Amy lots of questions until she had poured out the whole story.

Mr Stewart asked how the police had found out about Amy's and Lisa's adventure

'A member of the public saw them and informed Mr Jenkins, who reported the matter to us,' said the policeman. 'It's a very valuable horse, that one, and Mr Jenkins was very worried about it. Thank you for your help; we'd better go round to see young Lisa now. I suggest that in the future you and your friends be more careful what you get up to in your spare time. If that horse had kicked Lisa on the head she could well have been killed. There's a lot of power in a horse, you know. And you were trespassing, too.'

After the police had gone, Amy's parents were furious with her.

'Is that the sort of thing you get up to with Lisa?' asked Mr Stewart. Amy, who had stopped crying, started again as he went on, 'from now on I'm not having Lisa coming round here and you're not to go out with her after school or at weekends, do you understand?'

Amy stared at him, 'What, never again?' she asked timidly. Mr Stewart thought for a moment:

'Well, not for a few weeks at least, until I say it's OK.'

*　　　*　　　*　　　*　　　*

That evening Janet Corby was sitting in her bedroom. She was unaware of her neighbours' problems - she had one of her own to think about. She took the letter, in its blue envelope, from her bedside table to read yet again.

Dear Janet,

I don't know whether this will reach you but perhaps if you don't live at Withamby any more your parents will pass it on to you.

I know this letter will be a shock to you. It may be wrong of me to contact you after ten years but there is something important that I want to tell you. A year ago I became a Christian. Ever since then I have thought that I would like to get in touch with you again.

I know I am responsible for Sarah and that I should not have left you alone with her. Now that I'm a Christian I can see just how wrong I was and I want to apologise to you, and to Sarah.

In the past ten years I have done many things and have travelled about all over the world, but I never found what I was looking for until I met Jesus. Now I am living in a flat in Nottingham and working in an office. I go to a good church near here.

Please don't feel that you have to reply to this letter - I will understand if you don't. I don't want to upset your life in any way. You will probably be married by now and have other children. But please also know that I would be glad to hear from you, if you feel it's right.

With best wishes,
Richard.

Janet put the letter down. She didn't know what to do. Should she reply or not? And, if she did reply, what should she say?

Chapter Eight

The Holidays Arrive

July came, and with it the summer holidays. The hay was already baled and gathered in and now the crops were ripening fast in the fields. Harvest would soon be here. It was the time of year when everyone was talking about their holiday and one day Amy asked her mother whether they would be going to France or Spain. It was always one or the other.

'Ah yes, I meant to tell you,' Mrs Stewart replied. 'We wont go abroad this year. Instead we'll stay here and have some days out in the car. It will be a holiday at home!' Seeing Amy's surprised face she went on. 'There are lots of places we haven't seen yet, big houses and castles and a farm with rare breeds of animals. We can go to the seaside, if the weather's nice enough.'

Amy didn't think a 'holiday at home' would be as much fun as going to France or Spain but she did like the thought of castles - they sounded exciting.

Lisa said that she was going to Scotland with her family, they went every year and stayed in a big caravan at a caravan park, 'but not till after the Show.'

By the beginning of August, the villagers were busy preparing for the Withamby Show. It wasn't big or spectacular, but it was a traditional annual village event which most people went along to every year.

One cold, wet afternoon, two weeks before Show day, Sarah was sitting in the little living room looking at the rain spattering onto the window. Her mother was nearby, reading a book.

'Mum,' said Sarah, 'I'm bored.' Janet Corby looked up. For a moment it seemed as if she was about to say something important but then changed her mind. 'It's a shame you can't go into the garden. Just look at that rain, what terrible weather! Why don't you decide what you're going to do for the Show? You did well last year, coming second in the Childrens' Art competition.'

Sarah thought back to all the Withamby Shows she'd been to in the past. There were outdoor stalls, sports and games, and a Shetland pony for the little children to ride up and down on. If it was a fine day the show was a success, but if it was a wet day it was a failure. Everything depended on the weather. Sarah looked at the rain lashing down outside. 'I hope it's not like this on Show day,' she thought.

Sarah didn't know what to do for the show. She didn't want to start another painting but then she had an idea. 'Mum, could I make a cake for the baking competition, or am I too young?'

'No, I don't think you're too young, why not try? You're quite good at baking,' said Janet. Sarah took some recipe books down from the shelf and started to leaf through the sections on, 'Cakes and Biscuits.'

Janet, meanwhile, turned the pages of her book but she wasn't really reading it, she was thinking about Richard. In the end she had decided that she would write back to him. In the letter she told him about her mother dying, and then explained that she too had become a Christian.

She was rather shocked when Richard wrote back straight away. He sounded very happy to hear from her and said that he would like to come and visit her and Sarah! Now Janet didn't know what to do. She had been trying to think of a good way to tell Sarah about Richard but it was very difficult. Sarah had never seen her father before; would she would even want to know him?

After Richard's second letter had arrived, Janet decided that she should tell her father. Grandpa listened carefully, read the letters, and looked serious.

'You'd better think about it very carefully, Jan. After all, look how he treated you before. He says he's a Christian now, but you haven't seen him for ten years. You don't know what he's really like, do you? And you've got Sarah to consider.'

As Janet thought about what her father had said, a sudden miaowing noise interrupted her thoughts. Tabsy had pushed the door open with her paw and was wanting some food. Janet got up.

'Alright then,' she said to the cat, 'I'll get you something. You're always hungry these days!'

Sarah stroked Tabsy. 'Mum, do you think she's getting a bit fat?' Janet picked the cat up.

'You're right,' she said. 'Her tummy is big!' She felt Tabsy's stomach gently and then an idea struck her. 'I wonder whether she's having kittens?'

'Kittens!' exclaimed Sarah joyfully. 'Oh, great! Can we keep them?'

Janet laughed. 'I doubt it. Your Grandpa thinks one cat is quite enough!'

*   *   *   *   *

The day of the Withamby Show came at last. The weather was fine, although it was very windy. Sarah had made a big rich fruit cake and Grandpa had been busy preparing his vegetables. Together they walked to the Show Field carrying their precious exhibits carefully.

Inside the Produce Tent, Sarah laid her cake gently on a paper doyley on one of her mum's best plates. The cake looked lovely. Nearby, other people were arranging their displays of apples and chysanthemums, needlework and potato models, on the rickety wooden tables. When all was ready everyone had to leave, it was time for the judging. Outside the flapping marquee, Sarah and Janet saw a notice.

CHILDRENS' RACES

All age groups. 50m Dash, Egg and Spoon, Three-legged, etc. 2.30pm at bottom of field.

PRIZES

Janet thought it would be a good idea for Sarah to enter. 'Why don't you go along? You're good at sports.'

Sarah, Janet, and Grandpa walked round the field looking at the various stalls until, an hour later, the Produce tent re-opened after the judging. They hurried back inside to see whether they had won any prizes.

Grandpa went straight to the vegetable section and saw two rosettes by his vegetables. A red one, for first prize, for the potatoes and a blue one, second prize, for the runner beans. Although he didn't show his feelings he was secretly pleased. The other exhibitors slapped him on the back.

At the cake table, Sarah's fruit cake had been cut open and a small piece sampled by the judge. There was no rosette beside it but there was a card saying, 'Consolation.'

'Well done!' said Janet. 'You've got a consolation prize. That means that although your cake wasn't good enough to get first, second, or third, the judge liked it a lot.'

The Stewarts didn't go to the show until after lunch. As they came in through the gate, Amy spotted Lisa in the distance.

'Dad, please can I go and see Lisa?' she pleaded. Mr Stewart had been as good as his word, Amy and Lisa had not been allowed to play together out of school hours since the adventure with the horse.

Now he said, 'Well, I suppose you can't get up to too much mischief here. Alright, you can go. But I want you to meet us at the Refreshment Tent at half-past-three, do you understand?'

Amy ran happily over to Lisa and the two girls went into the Produce tent to look at the exhibits. At the cake table they saw Sarah's cake.

'Look at this!' said Lisa. 'Your neighbour has got a card for this mouldy looking cake. I wouldn't want to eat it for anything.' She wrinkled up her nose. 'She'll be really pleased with herself now or perhaps her Mummy made the cake and not her at all! Sarah sicky Corby really needs teaching a lesson.'

As it happened, Lisa's chance to 'teach Sarah a lesson' came sooner than she imagined. For at half-past-two, when she and Amy arrived at the bottom of the field for the childrens' races, Sarah was already lined up.

Chapter Nine

Finders Keepers

As Amy and Lisa came up to the starting line Sarah smiled and said, 'Hi,' but Lisa turned her back and wouldn't reply. Amy smiled back nervously then glanced at Lisa, hoping that she hadn't seen. Sarah, Amy, and Lisa were all to compete in the races for girls aged nine to eleven. There were ten other children waiting. Amy recognised some of them from her class at school. The first race, the 50m Dash, was about to start.

The thirteen girls stood at the starting line, waiting tensely for the 'crack' of the starting pistol. When it came, they raced off across the field towards a distant marker where a judge stood waiting to see who came first, second, and third.

Sarah took the lead. She was taller and older than most of the other children. Lisa, who had a lot of energy but short legs, watched helplessly as her enemy sped ahead. She tried so hard to catch up that by the time she crossed the finishing line, in third place, her face was flushed and her heart pounding. She looked so angry that Amy didn't dare speak to her.

It should have been fun climbing into the sacks and hobbling up to the starting line but Amy couldn't enjoy it now.

The man waited to fire the pistol again. 'Remember,' he said, 'you can jump or roll along or do whatever you like, but both feet must stay inside that sack!' He pulled the trigger and the girls were off again. It was so difficult that even Lisa smiled grimly, but that was only because she'd seen Sarah fall over.

Despite all Lisa's efforts she came third again. The only thing which made her feel better was that Sarah didn't come first this time, only second. But Lisa didn't really care about winning, she just wanted to beat Sarah.

While the girls were lined up waiting to start the Egg and Spoon Race, Lisa had an idea. At the sound of the starting pistol she was off like a shot. She dashed past Amy with her spoon gripped tight in front of her face. Her look of grim determination was so funny that Amy started to laugh and that made her drop her egg. She picked it up quickly but it was already too late; three other girls, including Sarah, had run ahead to catch up with Lisa.

Amy was concentrating so hard on keeping her egg on the spoon that she didn't see what happened ahead of her. As the little group of leaders neared the finishing line, Lisa saw that her enemy was going to beat her again. Quick as a flash, she knocked Sarah's elbow hard, sending the egg flying from her spoon. By the time she started running again Lisa was over the finishing line.

Amy was one of the last to finish. When she came panting up to Lisa she found that the judge was talking to her seriously. Lisa's face was like thunder.

'I'm sorry,' the judge was saying, 'but I saw you deliberately knock that girl's elbow so that she dropped her egg. I'm afraid you'll have to be disqualified. We can't have cheating, can we?' Lisa turned away, looking as if she was about to explode. Amy didn't dare go near her. She watched as Lisa, her face red and bitter, ran away as fast as she could, off up the field.

Amy looked first at Sarah and then at her friend disappearing into the distance, then she dashed after Lisa.

At half-past-three Amy went to the Refreshment tent to meet her parents and Charlotte. Lisa, who hadn't spoken since the Egg and Spoon Race, had already gone home. Amy didn't want to tell her mother and father about Lisa cheating; she thought they might stop her seeing her again.

'I'm tired,' said Mrs Stewart when they met up. 'Let's go in here and have a cup of tea.' Inside the big tent chairs and tables were set out, covered with cheerful red and white checked cloths. The Stewarts went over to the place where some ladies were serving tea, coffee, and home-made cakes. They turned to look for somewhere to sit and saw Janet nearby with Sarah. Janet beckoned and the Stewarts drew up some more chairs.

The marquee was nearly full and there was a gentle

hum of conversation in the warm, damp air. Amy and Sarah were embarrassed because of Lisa and didn't speak to each other. Sarah talked to Charlotte, who was full of all the things she'd seen and the Shetland pony she'd ridden on. Amy sat kicking the grass, tearing a paper napkin to shreds, and looking round the marquee at all the people.

After a while she saw Albert and Nelly come in. They bought some tea and cakes and sat down together at the far side of the tent. Mrs Stewart saw them too.

'How old is Albert now?' she asked.

'He's eighty - Nelly told me,' said Sarah. 'He's lived in the village all his life.'

'They used to know old Mrs Coverley who lived in your house until last year,' said Janet. 'It was Nelly who was friendly with her. Albert would never really speak.'

'Why not?' asked Mr Stewart. Janet smiled.

'As I understand it,' she said, 'it was because of something that happened years ago in the 1920's, at the time when Mrs Coverley got married. It was just a sad accident and not her fault at all, but Albert seemed to get it mixed up in his head and blamed her ever afterwards.'

Amy was listening intently now. She was very interested in Mrs Coverley and old Albert and his sister. Mr and Mrs Stewart asked what had happened.

'Well,' said Janet, 'Albert and Nelly were children at the time, about ten or eleven I think, and the family was quite well off in a small way. Their father was the village harness-maker; he made leather goods for horses. They lived down Brook Lane.'

Janet paused and glanced across at the old couple, 'Mrs Coverley or Miss Harris as she was then, was about fifteen years older than Albert and Nelly. It all happened on the day of her wedding. In those days, whenever there was a wedding, half the village turned out to watch the bride and groom come out of the church after the ceremony. Albert and Nelly went along to watch, too.

'They saw the new Mrs and Mrs Coverley get into their carriage and drive away but as soon as they were out of sight someone started shouting, saying there was a lot of smoke coming from the direction of Brook Lane. So everyone went to see what was going on and found that the Collins' house was on fire!

'People formed a human chain to get buckets of water from the stream to put the fire out. But it was too late for Mr Collins, he died inside the burning house. People said he must have been smoking his pipe and nodded off in his chair and that was how the fire started.'

'Oh dear, how awful!' said Mrs Stewart.

'It was sad,' agreed Janet. 'And I think Albert believes that if he hadn't gone to see the wedding, the fire would never have happened and his father wouldn't have died. Of course he might be right, but it wasn't his fault or Mrs Coverley's - it was just a tragic accident.'

'Those poor children,' said Mrs Stewart. 'What happened to their mother?'

'She got out of the house in time but Nelly told me that she never really recovered. She died about ten years later.'

They all looked over to where Albert and Nelly were sitting. 'Poor Nelly must have had a hard life,' said Mrs Stewart. 'First of all there was that fire, and then she had to look after Albert all these years.'

'Yes,' said Janet, 'and now he's got a bad heart, too.'

*   *   *   *   *

Back at home that evening, Amy asked her parents whether she could see Lisa the next day. If they'd known about the Egg and Spoon incident they would probably have said, 'No!'

'I suppose you can but I want to know exactly where you're going if you go for a walk, ' said Mr Stewart. After that, the girls were together again every day. By Thursday Lisa, who had been sulking since the village show, was in a better temper. The thought of her holiday cheered her up.

'We're setting off on Saturday morning, very early,' she said. 'Mum says we need to beat the traffic. I can't wait to get away from Withamby for a week, it's a real dump.'

The girls were on one of their favourite walks. It led along a path at the side of the cemetery and then down beside the stream which ran through the bottom part of the village. It was cool and shady under the trees beside the water and they sat down for a rest. Looking along the path into the distance they could see a paddock with two ponies, a brown one and a grey one, nibbling the grass. As they watched, the ponies looked up. They'd seen something, or someone. The girls saw someone too - it was Albert. Even though it was a nice warm day he was still wearing his black coat. He went up to the gate and started rummaging in his pockets for something to give his friends. The ponies ambled over and the old man patted them and stroked their manes.

'Let's follow him when he finishes talking to those ponies,' said Lisa. They waited quietly.

After five or ten minutes Albert strolled off. The girls got up and crept along under the trees until they came to the gate where he had been standing. The ponies were still there, watching them silently. Suddenly Lisa bent down and gave a little cry. 'What's this?' she exclaimed. 'A key!' The girls studied the big brass object in Lisa's palm.

'Albert must have dropped it when he was getting sugar out of his pocket,' said Amy, 'we'll have to give it back to him.'

'No!' said Lisa, 'he dropped it, *I* picked it up.'

'Lisa, you'll get into trouble again if anyone finds out and then I will too!' said Amy.

'You're really stupid!' said Lisa scornfully, 'look at it, does it look like a house key to you? It looks more like a *shed* key to me! *Understand*?' She stared at Amy, her eyes gleaming, 'What I say is, "Finders Keepers"!'

Chapter Ten

In the Night

Lisa examined the old key thoughtfully. 'I'll bet you anything it's the key to his coal-hole,' she said. But Amy wasn't so sure.

'Why should it be? He might just collect old keys, for all we know.' She wanted to forget the whole thing and give the key back to Albert. Being friends with Lisa was becoming too much trouble.

'I'll tell you what we'll do,' insisted Lisa. 'We'll go round there tonight after dark and find out whether this key opens the coal-hole door, OK?' Amy didn't like the idea one bit.

'No, not tonight I'm...I'm too tired,' she said.

'Alright, tomorrow night then, that's Friday.' Lisa's mind was working hard on her plan. 'That'll give me more time to arrange it, but it has to be tomorrow night because I'm going on holiday on Saturday morning.' She glanced up at Amy's miserable face.

'You're not getting out of it, Amy Stewart, or else I'll tell your Mum about you stealing money from her purse. You're coming with me.'

That night Amy was so worried that she couldn't get to sleep. Lisa's plan was going round and round in her head, making it ache. The next morning she was very quiet.

'Are you coming down with something?' her mother asked: 'You do look peaky.'

Friday arrived; each hour seemed to pass in slow motion, but at last it was bedtime. Amy was so nervous that she found it easy to stay awake. At half-past-ten she heard her parents coming up the stairs to go to bed. When Mrs Stewart tiptoed into Amy's room and stood by her bed for a moment Amy pretended to be asleep.

As soon as her mother had gone, Amy slipped silently out of bed and got dressed. At five-past-eleven she heard Lisa's secret signal, the sound of soil thrown against her window. She crept out onto the dim landing, glad that her parents left a night-light on. Their bedroom door was open a little but there was no sound from inside as she slipped past quietly.

Going down the staircase was terrifying, the stairs were old and wooden and very creaky. At the bottom Amy breathed a sigh of relief; she hadn't been heard. She lifted the old door latch and pushed gently, but as it opened, the door made such a loud noise that she froze on the spot. She held her breath, her heart pounding.

She waited for a minute but there was no sound from upstairs. Amy tiptoed into the kitchen, took the door key from its hook, slipped it into the lock, and turned it slowly. A few seconds later she was outside with Lisa.

Lisa put her finger to her lips and led the way around the end of the house. Only when the two girls were a distance away down Occupation Lane did they dare to whisper.

'I thought you weren't coming,' grinned Lisa.

'I had to go slowly down the stairs,' Amy replied, 'they creak!'

Although the night wasn't very dark Lisa was carrying a big torch; she explained it was for looking into the coal-hole. She seemed certain that the brass key would open the blue door.

As they approached Albert and Nelly's house they saw with relief that all the windows were dark. In silence the two girls hurried up the drive, trying not to make any noise with their feet.

At the back of the house they crept over to the coal-hole.

'You hold the torch,' whispered Lisa, 'and I'll try the door.' She pulled the big key from her pocket.

'Switch the torch on!' she ordered. Amy fumbled for the switch with trembling fingers. As she shone the beam at the lock, Lisa slid the key into the black keyhole. It revolved noiselessly. She gripped the door knob and turned slowly, the catch gave a 'click' and the door opened.

'Shine it in here!' Lisa whispered, and the two girls peered round the edge of the door into the black opening of the coal-hole.

'Wow!' breathed out Lisa slowly. 'Look at this lot!'
The back wall of the tiny brick room had shelves from floor to ceiling and they were loaded with a huge assortment of objects. Amy shone the torch up and down and along the rows. She spotted an old photograph of a man and a lady. The lady, sitting on a chair, was wearing a light high-necked blouse and a dark skirt which went down to the ground. Behind her stood the man, his beard dark and bushy. Amy wondered who the serious faced couple were. She noticed with surprise that everything in the coal-hole was strangely blackened.

The girls stood staring in silence. Then Amy shone the torch down to the floor. There were more things arranged around the walls; a rusty watering-can, some lumps of wood, some red roof tiles, and some pieces of twisted metal. In the corners there were still little piles of coal-dust left over from when the shed had been used for storing coal. There was also an old chair, its back broken off.

'I wonder if that's what Albert sits on when he does his "sorting out,"' thought Amy. But being reminded of the old man made her feel uneasy.

'Come on, Lisa,' she hissed, 'let's go!'

'Alright,' said Lisa, 'but let me get something from here first.' She reached into the coal-hole and took a tin from one of the shelves. She shook it and something heavy moved about inside.

'I wonder what it is? We'll find out later,' she whispered, tucking the box under her arm. She closed the door and turned the key silently in the lock. As Lisa slipped the key back into her pocket, Amy switched off the torch; she felt very relieved to be going home at last.

In the driveway between the two houses, Amy was just about to whisper goodbye when Lisa thrust the stolen tin into her hand. 'I've been thinking, you'd better keep this till I get back from Scotland.'

'What?' Amy hissed in horror. She didn't like the idea at all.

Above them, Sarah's window was wide open. When the whispering started below, Sarah woke up with a start. Thinking there might be burglars about, she crept out of bed in the dark and peeped out from behind the curtains. She was surprised to recognise the dark forms of Amy and Lisa in the driveway. They seemed to be arguing about something. She heard Amy say urgently. 'I don't want it Lisa, you take it!'

'No, Tommy might find it. Take it now!' Lisa replied.

In a few moments Amy disappeared round the back of the house. Lisa went off down the lane in the direction of her home. Sarah got back into bed but she lay awake for a long time, puzzling over the strange event. She was worried about Amy. Why was she outside at this time of night and what was it that she didn't want to take from Lisa? Sarah wondered whether she should tell anyone.

Meanwhile, next door, Amy crept back to her bedroom. She sat on her bed near the door. By the dim glow of the landing night-light, she studied the old tin. On the scratched and dented lid there was a faded picture of a smiling girl with lots of brown curly hair, holding a kitten. Normally Amy would have liked the picture, but not tonight. She tipped the tin to look at the lettering on the side, 'Chocolate Creams,' it said, but whatever was rolling around inside seemed heavier than biscuits. She put the tin down; she would wait until daylight to find out what was inside.

Amy looked round the room for somewhere to hide the tin and her eye fell on the bottom drawer of her dressing table. No-one would look in there.

'It's not fair of Lisa to make me take it,' she thought angrily as she slid the drawer open. 'She stole it, so she should have kept it!'

Lying safely back in bed, the visit to the coal-hole seemed like a bad dream. Amy wished with all her heart that she could put the tin back, but Lisa had the coal-hole key and now she was going away for a whole week.

'Besides, she'd be furious with me if I did that,' thought Amy, 'and she'd tell Mum about me stealing the money.'

What should she do? She lay there worrying, until exhausted, she fell asleep.

Chapter 11

The Old Tin

Amy slept in so late that her mother came to waken her. 'Come on, sleepy-head, it's a lovely day,' said Mrs Stewart cheerfully as she opened the curtains. 'We've all had breakfast already. Remember we're going to Langton today to buy your new uniform.

As her mother went downstairs Amy blinked in the bright morning light and then climbed heavily out of bed. With everything else that had been going on she had forgotten about the new school. She and Lisa would be starting at the same time... As she thought of Lisa, Amy remembered the events of the night before and glanced nervously at the bottom drawer of the dressing-table

She dressed quickly, wondering whether to open the tin. Now that everyone else was downstairs she had a chance to look inside if she hurried. She knelt down, opened the drawer, and lifted out the old, dented tin. Black stuff, like soot, smeared onto her fingers. She felt nervous about what she might find inside. Her hands were trembling as she gripped the lid.

The tin was lined with thin paper, yellowed and crisped with age. Amy lifted the flaps gingerly and saw a ball of filthy cloth. Whatever the heavy thing was, it was well wrapped up. She picked up the grubby bundle cautiously with the tips of her fingers; the cloth was knotted tight. As fast as she could, Amy unpicked the knots but found it inside another cloth. Now she could see circular things with sharp, curved edges, pushing through the grimy linen. She unknotted the second cloth and its contents spilled out onto the floor.

Amy gasped with astonishment. For out poured gold coins - lots of them, bright and shiny, rolling and gleaming in the bright sunshine on her faded bedroom carpet!

She gazed for a few moments in amazement and then reached out in awe to touch the treasure. She picked up a coin. On one side there was a man's head, he had a pointed beard and was going bald. On the other side there was a figure in a billowing cape riding a prancing horse and below that a date, '1902'.

'That's very old,' thought Amy. Then she realised with a shiver that the coins might be valuable.

The sound of her mother calling up the stairs made her scoop up the spilt gold hurriedly and tie it loosely in the cloths. As she stuffed the tin back into its hiding place she felt worried; things were worse than she had imagined. She knew it was a serious thing to steal something that was worth a lot of money. Whatever could she do? It wasn't right to keep the gold but she couldn't give it back now because she would get into trouble - big trouble!

Amy felt very lonely. The only person she could talk to about the treasure was now half way to Scotland. There was no-one else to turn to. She almost hated Lisa, this was all her fault!

* * * * *

Later, in Langton, Amy, Charlotte, and Mrs Stewart went to various shops and bought Amy everything she needed for starting at her new school. Mrs Stewart told Amy how nice it was that Sarah already went to the school.

'Janet said that she'll pass on outgrown things, it'll save us some money.' Amy pulled a face; she didn't like the thought of wearing Sarah's cast-offs - and what would Lisa say?

Normally Amy would have enjoyed the shopping trip - but not today. Life seemed as black as the inside of the coal-hole. Mrs Stewart was worried. 'She's not usually so quiet and miserable. I wonder what's the matter with her?' she mused.

At last they finished their shopping and decided to go home for lunch. On their way down the High Street they passed a small restaurant. Mrs Stewart glanced inside, then looked again and waved to some people who were sitting at a table by the window. As she walked on she said, 'That was Janet and Sarah with a man. I didn't recognise him. I wonder who he is?'

*   *   *   *   *

Inside the restaurant Janet and Sarah were having lunch
with Richard. Janet had at last told Sarah about him and
had been surprised by her calm reaction to the news.
'It'll take her some time to get used to the idea of
knowing her father again, after all these years without
one,' Janet thought.

Now the grown-ups were talking and Sarah was
watching the stranger. She had hardly spoken to him the
whole time, she was far too shy for that! Richard was
telling Janet about some of the things that had happened
to him in the past ten years, and his travels abroad. Sarah
tried to follow their conversation but she got lost somewhere between Australia and Malaysia! So she just sat
watching him. She had asked her mum what she should
call him, it didn't seem right to call him, 'Dad.'

'Just call him "Richard" to begin with,' Janet said.

He was quite tall with a thin face and short brown hair.
Like Sarah, he wore glasses. She wondered if she
looked like him, she thought he was quite handsome! He
had brought her a present, an address book and a nice
pen to go with it.

After lunch they went to the park. The sun came out
and it got hotter and hotter. As the adults alked on and
on, Sarah noticed how happy her mother looked.

There was a small cafe in the park which had tables
and chairs outside, shaded by big sun umbrellas. As they
walked past Sarah saw some children eating ice creams.
Richard followed her gaze, 'Would you like one, too?'
he asked.

A few minutes later they were all sitting under one of the green and white striped umbrellas, eating ice creams. 'Well, this is nice!' said Richard. He leaned back in his chair and beamed at them. 'In fact, this weather reminds me of the time when I first knew that God was trying to speak to me. It was a beautiful summer except for one very wet weekend!'

'We'd love to hear how you became a Christian,' said Janet.

Richard smiled. 'That's a long story,' he said, 'but I'll tell you how it all started.' He took a big bite of his ice cream thoughtfully. 'Funnily enough it was in Yorkshire! I'd travelled all over the world, trying to find out what the truth about life was, and then I first heard God speak to me in Yorkshire!' He threw back his head and laughed. 'I was on a walking holiday with my friend Dave. We'd walk all day, maybe fifteen or twenty miles, and stay in Youth Hostels at night. Well, one Friday evening we'd just reached the hostel when it started to rain. It poured, solidly all night and all next day, which was Saturday. It was so wet that we'd have got soaked to the skin if we tried to go anywhere so we stayed in the hostel.

'Now, Dave had been reading the Bible and we had long discussions about Christianity and other religions when we were out walking. I thought Dave was going a bit strange because he seemed to be interested in Jesus! I'd travelled a lot, you see, and I argued that all religions were the same. I didn't realise then that Jesus is the only way to God!'

Sarah, who had been so interested in Richard's

story that she had forgotten to eat her ice cream, let out a little cry. It was melting and running down her fingers.

'Lick it quickly!' said Janet, fishing in her pocket for some tissues. Richard went on.

'When we woke up on the Sunday morning we were really fed up to see that it was still raining! But we didn't like the thought of another day indoors so we decided to head for the nearest town to pass the time. When we got there at about ten o'clock there was nothing to do, as it was only a small place.

'We walked round until we saw some people heading off up an alleyway. We followed them, out of curiosity, and found ourselves outside a doorway. There was was sign on the wall saying, 'Christian Fellowship. Sunday morning meeting: 10.30am.'

'Come on, let's go in here,' Dave said.

'"No way," I said. "You go and I'll meet you later for lunch." But just then a man came up the alley.

'"'Ello lads," he said, all friendly and hearty. "Are you lookin' for the meetin'? You just go up them steps and turn right at the top."' Janet and Sarah smiled at Richard's imitation of the man's deep Yorkshire tones.

'I was completely trapped then. Even though I was dressed in my walking gear and my boots were a bit muddy I had no choice but to go inside! I didn't really like the meeting much. I wasn't used to church services and the people sang a lot of songs I didn't know. But when the pastor started to preach I felt as if God was speaking directly to me. What that pastor said made me feel unhappy because I remembered...' Richard paused and looked out across the sunlit flower beds, '...some of the things I'd been trying to forget.' He glanced at Janet and smiled.

'Well, I didn't become a Christian that day but what the man said made such an impression on me that when I got home I started to go to a church near where I lived. It wasn't too long before I became a Christian.'

'What about Dave? What happened to him?' Janet asked.

'Poor old Dave!' said Richard, 'the odd thing is that he's still not a Christian. Strange, isn't it?'

Soon it was time to go home. Janet, Sarah, and Richard arranged to meet in Langton again the following Saturday. On the way back Sarah was very quiet. But when Janet asked her what she thought of Richard she smiled.

'I think he's really nice, Mum.' Janet breathed a silent sigh of relief; she thought Richard was really nice too!

Chapter 12

'As for man, his days are as grass'

On Wednesday afternoon all was quiet at Number Six, Occupation Lane. Mr Stewart, his holiday over, was out at work. Mrs Stewart was in the living room, sewing. Charlotte was sitting at her feet, playing with her dolls. As she stitched, Mrs Stewart's mind was as active as her fingers. She glanced up at the old sampler on the wall, "As for man, his days are as grass,"' she read. It did seem a very dismal thing to put on a sampler, not at all cheerful! She looked up from her needle and thread and wondered about all the people who had lived in their cottage since it was built.

At that moment there was a knock at the door and she got up to answer it. Janet was standing outside.

'I'm at a loose end,' she said, 'so I've come round to see if you're free.'

'Come on in to the living room,' said Mrs Stewart happily. 'As a matter of fact I need cheering up. I'm feeling rather gloomy. I think it's because of reading the verse on that old sampler,' and she showed it to her friend.

'It doesn't make me feel gloomy,' Janet said, 'you see, I know the rest of that psalm!'

As Mrs Stewart was curious to hear what it said, Janet went quickly to fetch her Bible in order to show her friend Psalm 103.

'Here it is, it's one of my favourites,' Janet said when she came back, 'Look!' Together the two women studied the Bible, Janet explaining the meaning of the words. When they came to verse 17, she read out:

'"*But the mercy of the Lord is from everlasting to everlasting upon them that fear him, and his righteousness unto children's children.*"' Mrs Stewart was puzzled, so Janet explained, 'That means that although people don't live for long, God's love and mercy go on forever. He's so much greater than we are. This psalm is about how wonderful God is and how He looks after people who love and believe in Him. If we do, He forgives the wrong things that we've done, however bad we are.'

Janet was pleased to see how interested her friend looked. 'You see,' she went on, 'Jesus died on the cross so that we don't have to be punished. If we ask God to forgive us and if we accept what Jesus has done for us, we'll live with Him forever!'

Mrs Stewart had a great many questions about the psalm and about Jesus and the Bible. For some time she had been jealous of Janet's quiet contentment with life and was interested to learn about the cause of it. They talked for a long time and then Janet offered to lend her the Bible in order that she could read it later, on her own.

'I don't need this, I've got another one at home. Look, I'll put this marker in here for you, then you can find Psalm 103 easily.'

*　　*　　*　　*　　*

Meanwhile, upstairs, Amy was alone in her bedroom, examining the mysterious contents of the, 'Chocolate Creams' tin again. The coins were so shiny and interesting. On the side with the man's head there was some writing, 'EDWARDVS VII,' it said. She knew that 'VII' was '7' in Roman numerals and she worked out that, 'EDWARDVS VII' must have been King in 1902. There was some more writing, too, but she couldn't understand what it said. It seemed to be in a foreign language. Fascinating as the coins were, Amy wished she didn't have them; there was always a chance that someone would find them.

'Only three days till Lisa comes back,' she thought with relief, 'and then I'll tell her my plan.'

She put the coins away and went downstairs. Her mother heard her and popped her head round the living room door. 'Amy, I'm just having a cup of coffee with Janet. Will you go to the shop for me?' she asked as she searched in her bag for her purse. 'I need ten second class stamps and a pint of milk, can you remember that?'

It was a lovely day and Amy was glad to be outside. She strolled along, enjoying the warm sunshine and the singing of the birds. Things didn't seem so bad any more, not when she thought about her plan! She decided that she would go out with Lisa, after dark to return the gold, then give the old key back to Albert and Nelly the following day. They could say they'd found it, which was quite true. As she went past the pond the ducks quacked happily and dabbled in the silvery water; Amy already felt that the world was a happier place.

In the Post Office section of the shop she bought the stamps and then queued up at the till for the milk. She looked at the sweets; if she bought some with her mother's money and ate them on the way home no-one would know. But somehow she didn't feel like stealing, not any more.

As she waited to be served, she listened idly to two women chatting in front of her,

'It's Nelly I feel sorry for,' said one, 'she's a nice old lady and she'll be all on her own now.'

'I know,' said the other woman, 'it's such a shame for her, Albert was company, after all. Still, I heard he'd had a bad heart for a long time and he was eighty, I expect the funeral will be next Monday or Tuesday.'

Amy went cold. Albert dead? No, he couldn't be, but the woman had said his funeral was to be next week. Amy felt stunned, confused by a thousand horrible thoughts rushing through her head at once. Then an awful idea struck her, one that seemed too bad to be true, 'Albert found out that his gold coins were gone and the shock killed him!'

Somehow she managed to pay for the milk, and left

the shop in a daze. It was all too dreadful - now she was a murderer as well as a thief! The police would find out and come round again and then...she didn't know what would happen. Tears rolled down her face; she couldn't go home, she couldn't go anywhere!

She stumbled on until she reached the pond. She was so upset that she didn't notice Sarah coming in the other direction until she nearly bumped into her. Sarah was surprised to see Amy looking so unhappy. She felt so sorry for her neighbour that she put her arm round her shoulder, but that made Amy cry all the more!

'What is it?' Sarah asked gently, 'What's the matter?' She looked so kind and sensible and Amy was so desperate that she couldn't help pouring out the whole story.

Sitting on the railings by the pond she told Sarah all about Lisa finding the key, the secret visit to the coal-hole, and the gold coins hidden in her bedroom. She explained that she hadn't wanted to keep them but that Lisa had insisted. Sarah knew Amy was telling the truth and now she understood what had been going on under her window a few nights before.

'The worst thing is,' wailed Amy, 'that someone in the shop said Albert's dead!'

'Yes,' said Sarah, 'he died yesterday. Poor Nelly's very sad.'

'But you don't understand - Lisa and I killed him!' Sarah looked puzzled.

'Don't you see?' Amy went on, 'He died of a broken heart because his gold coins were gone. I'm sure he did!

What am I going to do?' She covered her face with her hands and sobbed helplessly as if her heart would break.

Sarah prayed silently, 'Lord Jesus, please show me what to do.' She thought for a while and then said in a quiet but decided voice, 'There's only one thing you can do.' Amy looked up at Sarah with hope.

'You have to tell your parents.'

'No!' Amy nearly screamed. 'I can't, they'll be furious with me and...what about Lisa?'

'You must tell your Mum and Dad,' insisted Sarah, putting her arm round Amy, 'and you must do it quickly or things could get a lot worse.'

Chapter Thirteen

Owning Up

Amy sat on the railing, sobbing miserably. In her heart she knew Sarah was right, she should tell her parents.

'But I can't face going home to tell my mum,' she wept.

Sarah had a suggestion. 'Pray to Jesus to help you.'

'Jesus?'

'Yes, that's what I'd do. He helps me all the time and He'll help you, if you ask Him. You can do it right now.'

Amy looked doubtful. 'What do you mean "pray"? How do I pray?'

'Oh, it's simple,' said Sarah. 'You just close your eyes and talk to Jesus as if He was sitting right beside you. In a way He *is* sitting right beside you, He listens to every word you say.'

But Amy was angry. 'That's silly! I'm not a Christian so why should He listen to me?'

'I used to think that,' said Sarah. 'Mum would tell me

to pray, but I thought it was a waste of time. I thought you could only tell Jesus about big important things, not about things like homework and people at school being nasty to you and your cat being ill! But it's not true. If you *really* want to know Him He'll start to speak to you, too.'

Amy looked up, red-eyed, 'What, you mean God speaks to you?'

'Oh yes,' said Sarah, 'He speaks to me and lots of people, only sometimes He says things we don't like to hear very much, so we ignore Him. Somtimes He speaks to me through the Bible or through other people. Once He told me I had to say sorry to Grandpa, he was cross because I'd broken one of his big flower pots. I felt awful but after I'd apologised I felt much better.'

'Well, I don't want to have Jesus telling me what to do!' said Amy crossly.

Sarah sighed. 'Perhaps I'm not explaining it very well,' she said. 'You see, you can trust Jesus. He won't ever let you down; He loves you so much that He died for you and He wants you to love Him. Because of Him you can go to heaven when you die and live with Him forever. But first you have to say sorry for all the wrong things you've done - and you have to mean it.'

Amy sniffed, 'But I'm *not* sorry and I'm *not* a Christian, so why should I bother about Jesus?'

Now Sarah looked worried. 'But Amy, you can't say that! Jesus died for everybody. It's the most important thing in the world to be a Christian.'

Amy, who could see that Sarah was serious, was

silent as her eyes filled with fresh tears. How she wished and wished that she had never been so friendly with Lisa. She felt as if everyone in the village knew what she had done and was talking about her. She wanted to run away somewhere and never come back. She knew that she had done some very wrong things and wondered whether what Sarah said about Jesus was true. What if it was true?

Amy glanced up and down the road to check that no-one was watching, then she bowed her head. In a short while she looked up. 'Alright then,' she said. 'I've asked Him to help me tell Mum but I don't see how He can sort this mess out.'

Sarah smiled and stood up. 'Come on then, let's go.'

The two girls set off along the pavement but Amy walked slowly, 'Please come to the house with me, Sarah,' she pleaded. 'I can't tell her without you being there.'

As they reached Occupation Lane Amy started to cry again. Sarah led her into the kitchen, told her to sit down at the table, and then knocked politely at the living room door.

Janet had gone home and Mrs Stewart was alone with Charlotte. She was surprised to see Sarah.

'Oh! Hello...' she began and then noticed Amy, her arms on the table and her head resting on them. Huge sobs were shaking her shoulders.

'It's alright, Mrs Stewart,' said Sarah. 'She's not hurt or anything like that, but she's very worried about something and she wants to tell you about it.' Mrs

Stewart went over to her weeping daughter, 'Come on then, let's all go and sit down in the living room where it's more comfortable.'

*　　　*　　　*　　　*　　　*

That evening when Mr Stewart came home, the story had to be told all over again. Although Amy cried she was surprised at how much of a relief it was to admit everything to her parents.

'Perhaps Jesus is helping me, after all,' she thought.

Her father examined the golden treasure carefully. 'They're sovereigns in quite good condition, too,' he said, turning one over in his hand. 'I'm fairly certain they're genuine. If they are, they must be worth quite a lot of money.' He weighed a coin in his palm, puzzled. 'Solid gold! But how did poor old Albert come to have all these in his outhouse? It's a real mystery!'

Mrs Stewart looked over his shoulder at the coins.

'That's Edward the Seventh, isn't it?'

'Yes, it is. He was the son of Queen Victoria; these coins were minted in 1902 that's the year Edward was crowned. He was only King for eight or nine years so there probably aren't many of them about. I wonder where Albert got them from?'

At the mention of Albert, Amy's eyes filled with tears again as she imagined the poor old man going to the shed and finding his precious treasure gone.

'Do we have to call the Police?' she asked timidly. Her father frowned; he was really quite cross with her.

'No,' he said slowly, 'but we'll have to see what Miss Collins has to say about it.'

'You mean Nelly?'

'Yes, tomorrow morning you're going to see her. You must apologise and give the coins back. Sarah knows Miss Collins well. I'll ask her if she'd mind going with you.' He sighed. 'You've certainly been very, very silly girls, you and Lisa. I just can't understand it, Amy, I just can't understand it.'

Then it was Mrs Stewart's turn to look sadly at her daughter. 'I wish we didn't have to trouble the old lady; poor Albert only died yesterday, after all, and she'll still be very upset.'

But Mr Stewart shook his head, 'I don't think we have any choice. This gold is hers and she should have it back straight away!'

*   *   *   *   *

The next day was Thursday. It was a sorry procession which made its way along Occupation Lane towards the little terrace of red brick cottages. Mrs Stewart went first and Amy and Sarah walked behind her. Amy had big black rings under her eyes she'd been worrying so much that she'd had very little sleep; Sarah felt sorry for her.

As they walked up the drive towards the brown door they heard the sound of an engine starting up at the back of the terrace. Then a lorry drove out past them, and away down the lane. Mrs Stewart knocked on the door and Nelly opened it almost immediately. She was wearing a round black velvet hat with a silver hat pin sticking out of it and she looked old and tired, but she smiled weakly when she saw the girls. Then she watched as the lorry disappeared round the bend in the lane and sighed softly.

'There it all goes...' she said, more to herself than to her visitors.

Mrs Stewart introduced herself and said, 'I heard about Albert, Miss Collins. I'd like to say how sorry I am; he was a very well-known figure in the village.'

'Thank you,' replied Nelly sadly: 'You're very kind. Would you like to come in?'

They all went through into the little living room and sat down. Amy noticed that the old photograph of the man and lady, which she'd last seen in the coal-hole, was propped up on the sideboard. Nelly saw her looking at it.

'Isn't it nice, dear? That's my mother and father. It was taken in the early nineteen hundreds, I think, just after they got married. I'm going to get it cleaned up properly, get all that soot off, they can do marvellous things with old photos these days, you know.'

She turned to Mrs Stewart, 'I've only just got the photo, you see. It's been in a shed for seventy years. Did you notice that lorry when you arrived? I asked the Council to come and clear out the coal-hole. Albert had a load of old things in there rubbish mostly, but it was his pride and joy. I wanted it cleared out because I didn't like to think of it all there when he's...when he's gone,' and Nelly's eyes filled with tears. She took out a hankie to dab them, 'Yes, it was mostly rubbish, but then I saw that old photo. I didn't know he had it but I thought I'd like to keep it as a souvenir.'

Mrs Stewart took a deep breath, 'Actually, Miss Collins, we've come round here to talk to you about the coal-hole.' And then she explained what had happened, leaving out some of the details because she didn't want to upset the old lady more than was necessary. But Nelly's eyes grew wider and wider.

'Well, just think of that!' she kept saying.

Then it was time for Amy to apologise for her part in taking the key and breaking into the coal-hole. It wasn't easy for her and when she had finished Nelly said, 'Oh dear, you did go off the rails, didn't you? But it's right that you came to see me about it. I can see that you really are sorry.'

Mrs Stewart had told Amy not to mention the sovereigns; she wanted to tell the old lady herself so as not to shock her. 'Do you know whether Albert had anything valuable in the coal-hole?'

Nelly shook her head. 'Oh no, I don't think so. Of course, I never looked in there but it was just old things, most of them broken.'

'Well, I'm afraid the girls took some things out of the coal-hole and I think they might be quite valuable.' Nelly's mouth fell open in surprise as she pulled a small, grubby parcel from her pocket.

'All that soot - just look at it!' she muttered as Mrs Stewart unwrapped the cloths, then laid them and the gleaming coins in her lap. Nelly gasped in astonishment.

'Well I never, sovereigns! I haven't seen any of these for years, she said and sat and stared at the shining gold.

She was too surprised to listen to Mrs Stewart telling her that she had a friend who knew about old coins. And when she asked her whether she could take one of the sovereigns to find out how much it was worth, Nelly just whispered, 'Oh yes dear, take as many as you like!'

But at last the old lady could think and speak straight again, 'It's amazing, Amy! Just think of it, if you hadn't taken these sovereigns out of the coal-hole they'd be gone in that lorry by now and be thrown down a tip and then we'd never have seen them again!' Suddenly she giggled. Everyone stared at her in surprise.

'What a good thing Albert doesn't know what I nearly did, giving his gold to the men from the Council!'

Nelly made them all a cup of tea, 'to recover,' as she said, and as they drank it she told them about Albert's illness.

'It was last Thursday that he took really ill. He went to bed and never got up again.' She wiped her eyes. 'It was his heart, of course. He never would take those tablets. He went out for his usual walk on Wednesday and then on the Thursday he took to his bed.'

Amy looked at Sarah. 'So,' she asked slowly, 'Albert didn't know that we'd been into the coal-hole on Friday night?'

'Oh no, dear. On Friday morning I called the doctor. Albert didn't want me to, but I insisted. He certainly never got out of bed after that, let alone outside, so he couldn't possibly have known anything about it. He can't even have known that he'd lost the key or he'd have been fretting about it.'

Amy felt as if a huge black weight which had been pressing down on her had been lifted. Albert hadn't known about the theft of the gold sovereigns after all! It wasn't the shock which killed him, just a natural illness. She felt so relieved but also very sad. It was strange to think that when she and Lisa had spied on Albert talking to his friends the ponies, it was the last time he ever saw them. Had he known that he was saying 'goodbye' for ever?

Albert, who had walked round the village all his life and knew it so well, was now dead and gone. Suddenly Amy remembered the Bible words on May Harris's old sampler. 'As for man, his days are as grass...For the wind passeth over it, and it is gone.'

Mrs Stewart, Sarah, and Amy left Nelly at last, saying they'd be back to see her soon. As they walked off down the lane they all felt much better.

Sarah thought how much happier her new friend looked, then all of a sudden she remembered something. With all the trouble, she'd forgotten to share some good news!

'I've got something exciting to tell you,' she said happily. 'Tabsy has had kittens!'

Amy's eyes lit up with delight. 'How many?'

'Three, two are just like her and there's a little black one, too. They're so sweet! Come and see them. Tabsy's got them in a box in the kitchen.'

The kittens were tiny; their eyes were tight shut.

When Amy and Sarah picked them up they waved their little paws helplessly in the air and mewed pathetically. Then Tabsy looked so worried that the girls had to give the kittens straight back to their proud mother.

Amy was so excited about the new arrivals that it wasn't until she was in bed that night that a thought came to her. 'What about Lisa?' It was only two days till she came back from her holiday in Scotland!

Chapter Fourteen

Lisa Comes Back

On Saturday, Janet and Sarah went to Langton to have lunch with Richard. Sarah had been looking forward to seeing her father again. This time she was less shy and told him all about the three new kittens. Now it wasn't just the two grown-ups who did all the talking! When it was time to say 'goodbye' they agreed that on the following Saturday Richard should come to Withamby for lunch. Grandpa, who was still worried about his daughter and grand-daughter, wanted to meet him.

That evening, after tea, Amy was sitting on her bed. She looked round the room, relieved that the old biscuit tin was no longer hidden in the dressing-table drawer. She was glad, too, that things had worked out so well. What a surprise it had been to find that, in the end, Nelly was actually pleased that she and Lisa had stolen the gold! 'Perhaps Jesus sorted it out for me,' Amy thought. She was beginning to learn that she could trust Jesus.

It had been an eventful week. First, Amy had helped Lisa to steal the sovereigns, then Albert had died, and now the treasure was back where it belonged - with Nelly. And there were the new kittens to think about. So much had happened since Lisa went away. The thought of seeing Lisa again made her feel nervous and uncomfortable. She looked restlessly out of the window and saw that Sarah was in her room next door. Amy opened the window and called to her friend.

It was very pleasant, leaning out into the warm evening air, chatting. First Amy asked about the kittens and then she told Sarah her worries about Lisa. 'She's coming back tonight and I just know she'll be round here tomorrow morning to see me. What shall I do?'

Sarah looked thoughtful as Amy went on. 'She doesn't know what was in that biscuit tin - she went off to Scotland before we opened it. She'll be furious when she finds out it was gold sovereigns - and that I've given them back to Nelly!'

Sarah looked sympathetic. 'I don't know what you can do. The best thing is to pray about it again.'

'Alright, I'll ask Jesus to help me. Please will you come round tomorrow morning when Lisa comes?' Without realising it, Amy had become dependent on her new friend. But Sarah had other plans. 'I can't; I'm going to church. Why don't you come? There's a Sunday School.'

Amy thought for a moment: 'I'd like to - but I want to explain everything to Lisa. I should stay here and see her. But I'll come next week, if Mum and Dad let me.'

*　　*　　*　　*　　*

At 9.45am the next morning Amy saw Sarah and Janet setting off for church. After they'd gone she felt lonely and wished she was with them, but she knew it was right to stay behind. She sat nervously in the kitchen, waiting. Mr and Mrs Stewart and Charlotte were in the living-room, Amy had told her parents that she wanted to see Lisa alone. The time passed slowly and Amy was very relieved when at last she heard Lisa's knock. Her friend came into the room grinning; she looked brown and full of beans after her holiday.

Straight away she burst out, 'My Mum just found out about Albert dying - I suppose you've heard. Serves him right if you ask me!' and she laughed loudly. Amy was shocked at Lisa; she hadn't realised before how horrible her friend was.

Lisa noticed Amy's expression and could tell that something was wrong. Amy would normally have sniggered along with her - so why did she look so glum now? Lisa's grin faded in an instant.

'What's the matter with you?' she asked crossly. Amy looked at the floor; she couldn't speak. Then Lisa remembered something, 'Oh! I nearly forgot about Albert's old tin. What's in it?' Amy tried to pluck up courage to tell Lisa what she'd done - and was surprised to find it was easier than she thought. Jesus must be helping her again.

'I haven't got it any more. What we did was wrong - we shouldn't have stolen Albert's things.' Lisa's look of scorn made her feel uncomfortable, but Amy went on,

'There were coins in that tin, Lisa - real gold ones worth a lot of money.'

Lisa exploded, 'Don't say you've sold them!'

'No - I gave them back to Nelly.' Lisa was silent at last. She was too surprised to speak but her face showed all her feelings: anger, contempt, greed, hatred - but mostly anger.

'What on earth did you do that for, you...' and she called Amy a lot of rude names. When she ran out of bad things to say she said, 'Why didn't you wait till I got back and then you could have given them to me instead, if you wanted to get rid of them?' Amy tried to explain.

'But it was wrong to keep them, and anyway, when I heard that Albert was dead I thought he'd found out and died of shock.'

As Amy had expected, Lisa was getting more and more furious and now she got up and stormed to the door, snarling, 'So I suppose you felt sorry for him, then? You always were pathetic. I hate you! And I don't want to see you ever again!'

Despite Lisa's anger Amy felt calm. 'But we'll have to see each other at school,' she said.

'Then I won't speak to you and I'll tell everyone...' Lisa's voice tailed off as she realised she couldn't tell anyone anything without giving herself away. She went out, slamming the door hard. The room shook and rattled and then there was silence. It was all over.

Amy started to cry - but it was with relief. She could see now just how nasty Lisa was and she didn't want to be like her. She wondered how she could have been

Lisa's friend for so long. Then, deep in her heart a small voice said: 'You were friends with Lisa because you were like her, inside!'

Amy looked up at the kitchen clock to work out how long it would be before Sarah came home. After lunch she could go round and tell her all about what had happened. The thought of seeing Sarah made Amy happy - they were such good friends now. Amy wondered why she had ever disliked her neighbour.

*   *   *   *   *

Monday was spent mainly in getting ready for school on Tuesday. At lunchtime Amy asked her mother whether she could have one of Tabsy's kittens, when they were old enough to leave their mother. She knew what Mrs Stewart's answer would be.

'I'm sorry Amy, but we don't want a cat. The food is expensive and they're a lot of work and trouble.'

Despite that disappointment Amy was excited about going to the secondary school in Langton. Even though Sarah was in the year above, they'd be able to sit together on the bus and see each other in the breaks.

The next morning the two girls walked along the road to the bus-stop. The bus came in a few minutes and Amy saw at a glance that Lisa was already on board, sitting alone at the back. As Amy and Sarah walked up the aisle and sat down together Amy felt Lisa's eyes, watching her.

'She hates me now,' said Amy as she sat down, 'and I hate her too!'

Sarah smiled. 'Jesus doesn't want you to hate her - He wants you to love her and pray for her - perhaps she'll become a Christian.'

Amy was doubtful. 'Lisa? She's far too horrible to be a Christian!'

'No, she's not,' Sarah said firmly. 'We're all bad in different ways. If she's really sorry for all the awful things she's done God will forgive her too. It would be a miracle if she did become a Christian, wouldn't it...?' She broke off and laughed, 'but then miracles are no problem for God!'

Amy found all this hard to believe, and even wondered if it was fair that God should love someone like Lisa. But she decided to pray for her, all the same.

Sarah went on, 'You see, Jesus died for us, even though He can see what we're really like inside. He wants to change your heart so that you can love people like He does.

Then Amy remembered Lisa's threat. 'But she said she'd tell people at school about me,' she complained, 'what if no-one likes me?'

'Don't worry,' said Sarah. 'I've got some friends and they'll be your friends, too. As the bus trundled on up the hill and out of the village, Amy thought about what Sarah had said. She knew that Lisa had been wrong about everything. And she could tell that what Sarah said was true. She glanced back between the seats to where Lisa was sitting, and then at Sarah.

She took a deep breath and whispered, 'I think I do want to be a Christian, Sarah.'

Chapter Fifteen

The 'Thank You' Tea Party

'Here you are, Miss Collins,' said Mr Stewart as he handed Nelly a thick wad of notes, 'the sovereigns have been sold and this is the money for them. It's all yours!'

Nelly's eyes widened as she took the notes, 'I've never seen so much all at once, just think of it - hundreds of pounds!'

The whole Stewart family, as well as Grandpa, Janet, and Sarah, were crammed into Nelly's little sitting room. The old lady was wearing a cheerful hat made of orange feathers to honour the occasion. Plates of cakes, sandwiches, scones, and sausage rolls were laid out on the table. Nelly explained that there wasn't room for them all to sit round the table, 'but I'm sure you won't mind a plate on your knees, will you, dears?'

It was more than a month since Albert's death. Nelly had invited the two families to tea to say, 'thank you' for the help they'd given her.

'You've all been so good, what with popping in to see me and looking after me and you went to all that trouble to sell the sovereigns,' she said, smiling at Mr Stewart.

Getting up, she went over to the sideboard where the old photograph of her parents stood in pride of place. Nelly pulled open a drawer and took out something very small, which was wrapped in a piece of tissue paper.

'I nearly forgot. This is for you, dear,' she said, handing the little parcel to Amy with a grin at Mr and Mrs Stewart. 'Your Mum and Dad may not think you deserve it, but if it hadn't been for you, I'd never have had all this,' and she waved the banknotes in the air.

Amy unfolded the tissue and found one of the gold sovereigns inside! She looked up at Nelly in surprise.

'Oh, but I can't take this!'

'Yes dear, please do. I've got enough money here, I can spare one of them.

Amy turned the sovereign over and over in her hand, it gave her a funny feeling to see King Edward's profile and the bareback rider again! She would keep the gold coin forever as a reminder of the worst time of her life, and the best.

'It's very kind of you to give Amy that sovereign, she doesn't deserve it,' said Mrs Stewart, 'but what are you going to do with the money you got from selling the others? Have you got any plans?' Nelly thought for a moment.

'Most of it's going in the bank but with the rest I'll do something I've been wanting to do for years!' and she grinned at their curious faces. 'I'm going to Bridlington to see my cousin. I went once, years and years ago, and we had a lovely time; I love the seaside. But with Albert being, you know how he was, I couldn't very well leave him for long. But now I'm free...' and she sighed sadly.

Soon they started their meal. Nelly served them tea in her best cups.

'It's not every day I have such a lot of visitors,' she said happily. As they ate, Janet asked her about the sovereigns and whether she knew where Albert had got them from.

'Well, it's funny you should ask that,' said the old lady. 'You see, Mr Stewart brought them round just after Albert died and I was too upset to bother much about them. So it wasn't until last week that I was thinking back to the old days and I remembered something that I hadn't thought of for seventy years!' She nodded towards the old photograph on the sideboard.

'It all started when I got that picture back from the restorers. It reminded me of when we were children, Albert and me, and our house down Brook Lane. That was before the fire of course, the house was burnt out and my father died, you know.

'Anyway, I remembered that we had a fireplace in the kitchen with a great high mantelpiece, well it looked high to me because I was just a little tot then. There was a thick plank of wood along the top as a shelf and some nice old-fashioned tiles down the sides, too. On top of the mantelpiece Father kept an old teapot I can see it now, blue and white it was, one of those Chinese style patterns. I think it must have been a wedding present.

'Now...' and Nelly leaned forward in her chair to look at them seriously, '...I'm fairly sure he kept his sovereigns in that old teapot. I've got a dim memory of being told there was something special in it. My guess is that every time he got one he put it in there, it was a sort of piggy bank. Sovereigns were worth a pound each, you know, and that was a lot of money in those days.' The old lady fell silent remembering those faraway times with a dreamy look in her eyes.

Mrs Stewart was puzzled. 'But if the house burned down, wouldn't the sovereigns have been lost in the fire?'

Nelly smiled. 'Well, I suppose Albert must have found them, somehow or other. But it's a wonder they didn't all melt and run away into the ground, isn't it?' She giggled and went on, 'Albert was a funny boy. After we moved in here with my mother, he'd go back to Brook Lane to where the old house had stood, and go through the rubble, poking and digging about. He'd be down there every few days for years afterwards. At that time there were still one or two walls standing but they've all fallen down now. Albert was always bringing bits and pieces back. Everything broken and covered in soot so my mother and I made him put the stuff straight into the coal-hole. He put shelves up one year, to store it all, and in the end the place was full of all that rubbish.'

'And the sovereigns!' added Mr Stewart. Nelly laughed. 'Yes, and the sovereigns. I never guessed he'd found anything as valuable as that!'

Now Amy understood the coal-hole had been Albert's secret store for all the things he'd saved from the burnt out house in Brook Lane.

Later, Sarah and Amy told Nelly about the kittens; the little animals had their eyes open now and were very playful. The old lady was delighted.

'Oh, how lovely. I do like babies of any variety!' Grandpa invited her round to see them;

'I'd be really pleased if you'd have one of them, I don't want four cats in the house!' he said.

'They're a month old now,' added Janet. 'They'll be big enough to leave Tabsy before too long.'

'And then what will happen to them?' asked the old lady.

'I don't know. We have to find homes for them, somehow,' said Janet. Nelly looked thoughtful.

'Do you know, Jack?' she said at last to Grandpa, 'Perhaps you're right - perhaps I should have a kitten. Did I hear you say there was a little black one? I've been lonely since Albert died and it would be company for me, wouldn't it? It will be winter soon, too, and the mice will be coming back.' On hearing that, Mrs Stewart looked worried.

'What do you mean? All our mice went away in the spring when the weather got warmer. Do you think they'll come back again?'

Nelly laughed. 'I'm afraid so, my dear. When the colder weather comes there's nothing for them to eat outside and so they try to get back into the houses.'

'Oh dear,' said Mrs Stewart, 'what shall we do?'

114

Amy smiled at Sarah. 'We could have one of Tabsy's kittens! She's a very good mouser so her kittens probably will be too.

Mrs Stewart looked at her husband, 'What do you think?' she asked. Mr Stewart smiled.

'Well, I suppose a cat would be useful for catching those mice and the girls would like it too.'

'Alright then, we'll have one,' said Mrs Stewart with a sigh. Charlotte started to dance around the room with joy. Amy was just as excited and started to think of a good name for the kitten.

But there was yet another surprise to come that evening. After tea, when they were sitting chatting, Janet said, 'I've got an announcement to make!' and she grinned at Sarah and Grandpa, who grinned back; it was obvious they had a secret to share. Mrs Stewart was very curious to know what it was. 'Come on, Janet,' she laughed, 'Hurry up and tell us!'

'Well,' said Janet, 'I'm getting married!' The others were so surprised that for a few moments no-one said anything. It was Nelly who spoke first.

'How lovely dear, but who's the fellow?'

Then Mrs Stewart remembered the man in the Langton restaurant; she'd seen him visiting the house next door several times since then.

'Is it the man with the blue car?' she asked. Janet laughed.

'Yes!' She nudged Sarah: 'Tell them who he is!'

'He's my Dad!' said Sarah.

Everyone started to talk at once, they were all so

pleased and happy for Janet and Sarah.

'Well I never, just think of it! He's turned up again after all these years. He must have had a change of heart and no mistake,' said Nelly. She waved the wad of banknotes at Janet.

'And now I'll be able to buy you a lovely wedding present, dear! Won't that be nice?'

Chapter Sixteen

Flowers of the Field

In a few weeks time the kittens were old enough to leave Tabsy. Nelly took the little black one, she'd already given it the name, 'Sooty.' Janet was sure that Sooty would be spoilt. The old lady had already bought lots of tins of the best food for him! The Stewarts had one of the tabby ones and in the end it had been Charlotte who had chosen his name, 'Tigger.' The Corbys couldn't find a home for the third kitten, Twinkle, and so Sarah was allowed to keep her. Sarah and Amy were very happy, they'd have a kitten each.

The Stewarts had never kept a cat before and so Sarah had to explain to them how to look after Tigger and how to house train him. Mrs Stewart grumbled, 'All this money for food and cat-litter, not to mention the bother of it just for one tiny kitten!'

But soon she loved Tigger just as much as Amy and Charlotte did; he was always making them laugh. Even so, Mrs Stewart was firm about one thing. 'That cat is not going upstairs - I'm not having him climbing all over the beds!' As Tigger was to sleep in the kitchen, Mr Stewart made him a bed from a box and the girls lined it with one of Amy's old pullovers, to keep the kitten warm.

They'd only had Tigger for a few days when Mr Stewart came home from work much earlier than usual one afternoon, looking very pleased about something. He explained that he'd been called to a business meeting at which the manager had given him some good news.

'What is it, what did he say?' Mrs Stewart asked impatiently. He smiled,

'Well, now I'm on a "basic salary plus commission basis"!' he said. Amy didn't understand this but she saw that her mother was delighted.

'What does it mean?' Amy asked.

Mrs Stewart replied, 'It means that we get a little bit more money! I wonder...?' she said, half to herself, 'I wonder if we could think about buying this cottage now?' They had a special tea that evening to celebrate Mr Stewart's pay rise and even Tigger had a new tin of food.

Janet was busy planning her wedding. It was to be a quiet, private one - just family, friends from the church, the Stewarts, and Nelly were invited. Amy and Sarah were excited because it had been arranged that, while Janet and Richard went on their honeymoon, Sarah was to stay with Amy. Afterwards, Richard would come to live in Withamby.

The first time Grandpa had met Richard for himself he saw that he could be trusted. And Grandpa was happy to have his new son-in-law living in the cottage although, as Janet said, 'The house will be so small with four of us in it. I think we'll have to have an extension built on at the back to give us more room!'

Now, Amy went to church every week with Janet and Sarah. She enjoyed the Sunday school and was learning something new every week. She had her own Bible now and, helped by Sarah, she was getting to know and love Jesus more and more.

Mrs Stewart, too, was reading the Bible. She knew now that God had arranged for the family to come to Withamby and she had grown to love her new life. She realised that there were things more important than a big, comfortable house and a lot of money; she knew that God wanted her to trust Him to arrange things in the best way for her and her family,

'It's as the old sampler says,' she sometimes thought, 'We're all like the flowers of the field. One day we'll be blown away like seeds on the wind, so we should make good use of our time while we have it.'

*　　*　　*　　*　　*

One afternoon towards the end of October, Lisa Ross and her mother Marilyn were walking up Occupation Lane towards the village. Lisa was moodily kicking up the brown and yellow autumn leaves which lined the pavement.

As the pair approached the red brick terrace where Nelly lived, Lisa walked faster. She had too many bitter memories of the old lady's cottage and didn't want to be reminded of them. But, as they passed by, a figure in the front garden straightened his back. It was Grandpa.

'Afternoon, Jack,' called Marilyn, 'are you helping Nelly out?'

'Yes,' said Grandpa, 'I'm just tidying up the garden before winter sets in.'

When they were far enough away, Marilyn muttered, 'So, Jack Corby's doing Nelly's garden now! I heard that those Corbys were getting friendly with her - perhaps they're hoping she'll leave them something in her will. She's got no children, after all.' Then a thought struck her: 'Mind you, though, I don't expect she's got much money!'

Lisa was silent as they walked on in the fading light. But as they came up to the twin stone cottages Marilyn asked, 'Are you still not speaking to Amy Stewart?'

'No!' Lisa snapped angrily. 'I'm never going to speak to her again.' Marilyn shrugged.

'I've heard about that lot,' and she jerked her head towards the two cottages, 'they're as thick as thieves now - and fancy Sarah's Dad turning up again after all these years!'

'Huh!' grunted Lisa moodily, but she looked wistfully across the road at Amy's house. The curtains were shut and wispy smoke was drifting from a chimney up into the still evening air. In her heart Lisa wished she was still friends with Amy, although she doubted that Amy would want to be her friend again. 'I suppose I did say a few nasty things to her, but these days she's always with sicky Sarah and that creepy crowd at school,' she thought.

But, as Lisa followed her mother through the deepening dusk, she wondered whether it might not be better to have Amy, Sarah, and a 'creepy crowd' as friends, than to be as she was now with no friends at all. She sighed. It was hard to swallow her pride.

'Perhaps I'll say something rude to Amy tomorrow at school, just to see if she will talk to me again.'

In her heart she had a feeling that Amy would.

*If you enjoyed this book
you will be pleased to know
that there are other books
in the Fulmar series*

Find out more...

WINNER OF THE
CHILDREN'S BOOK CHALLENGE

ARABELLA FINDS OUT

by Jaqueline Whitehead

'The screams and giggles were deafening and the whole place seemed full of wet hysterical children.

Arabella's father, hearing the noise from his study came outside. He looked in utter disbelief at what was going on and then shouted angrily at the top of his voice...for the first time in her life, Arabella felt frightened - everthing was horribly out of control.'

Arabella hopes the party on her estate will impress her new friends. When her plans do not turn out as she expected she realises that being rich can cause problems. She begins to find out that her friends possess something which money can't buy. However, she is in for another shock when her father makes a terrible discovery.

ISBN 1-85792-161-5

Sample Chapter

1

Arabella was rich. In fact she was very, very, rich, at least her father was, and that meant she was too. At one time her father had been poor, but he didn't like it much. So he bought things that were cheap and nasty and sold them for too much money to anyone who would have them. Things like plastic Big Bens that played, "Maybe it's because I'm a Londoner", which were very popular with Japanese tourists, and Solar powered torches which were a big hit with Eskimos. Strangely enough, by selling things like these he became rich quickly. By the time Arabella was born, he had quite forgotten what it felt like to be poor.

Arabella was quite used to telling off the servants, being rude to the gardeners and ordering Hargreaves the chauffeur to drive through enormous puddles just after he had spent all morning waxing the Bentley. Arabella didn't go to school but had a private tutor called Miss Marshall who came to the house on Mondays, Tuesdays, Thursdays and Fridays. On those days Arabella would go upstairs to the school room for her lessons. These were not a great success because when Miss Marshall said, 'Good Morning, Arabella, please open your books,' Arabella would shout, 'No, go and buy me some sweets.' Miss Marshall had a twitch.

When Arabella was nine her mother said to her one

morning at breakfast, 'Darling, I think it is time you went to school.'

'What!' said Arabella.

'Don't say what,' said her father, his mouth full of buttered croissant and french coffee. 'Say pardon.'

Arabella glared at her father and shouted, 'What! What, what, what, what, what!' and pulled a face at him. Then she shrieked at her mother, 'I don't want to go to school, I want to stay at home with Miss Marshall.'

'Miss Marshall is not a very good teacher,' said her mother. 'What is three and three?'

'Eight,' yelled Arabella.

'Good grief,' said her father. 'It's definitely time you went to school.' He was good at sums because he was used to counting all his money. He smiled at his wife. 'Have you a school in mind, my dearest?'

'Yes, I have,' she replied. 'Lady Worthington's Educational Establishment for rich, genteel young womenfolk.'

'Sounds ideal,' said Arabella's father. 'Why not give them a call after breakfast?'

'I did think we might take a drive over there this morning and have a chat with the head,' suggested Arabella's mother.

'Even better,' said Arabella's father warmly. 'It is Hargreaves' day off but I could drive us, it would make a pleasant change. We could stop and have lunch at Luigi's.'

'That's settled then,' said Arabella's mother, 'I'll go and get ready.'

125

'I don't think we had better take, 'you know who,' this time do you?' said Arabella's father nodding at Arabella in a very obvious way, but one which he clearly believed she wouldn't notice. Arabella's mother nodded back to show she agreed completely with the wisdom of this. 'We won't take you this time Snookums,' he said to Arabella, 'you can come and see your new school the next time we go.'

'Dadsy.' Arabella spoke in a soft wheedling tone. 'Snookums doesn't want to go to school.'

'I know,' he replied. 'But I'm afraid this time Snookums will have to trust that Mumsy and Dadsy know best.'

Arabella reverted to her old self.

'I don't want to go to school! I don't want to go to school! I don't want to go to school! I don't! I don't! I don't!' she screamed. After yelling blue murder for three minutes, holding her breath until she turned grey and threatening to be sick, Arabella gave up, realising this time Mumsy and Dadsy had made up their minds. How they must hate her to make her leave home every day to go to school.

Arabella flounced off feeling very cross and frustrated. No one understood her, no one cared, she didn't matter. As these thoughts took hold she began to feel very sorry for herself. Two big tears rolled down her cheeks and she stopped flouncing and became like a heroine in a tragedy. Suddenly with dramatic effect she flung an arm across her face and ran sobbing to the summer house in the east gardens hoping all the way that someone would see her performance and come to comfort her. There she threw herself to the floor and gave in to what she hoped was 'abandoned sobbing'. Arabella had read about it in a romantic book she'd found in Miss Marshall's bag when she was looking for peppermints and liked the sound of it. Miss Marshall never did find out where her book had gone, nor the peppermints for that matter.

Arabella sobbed as loudly as she could hoping all the time that her parents would hear and realise how cruel they were being but instead she heard the car start at the front of the house and pull away down the drive. She stopped sobbing. What a cheek they hadn't even come to say goodbye. She pouted sorrowfully, 'I'm all alone, with no one to care for me.' She said the words out loud and liked the feel of them. In fact there was a house full of staff, so she wasn't alone at all, but the thought suited Arabella's mood. At this she considered another bout of abandoned sobbing. As there was no one around to appreciate it she didn't bother and instead hauled herself up off the floor onto the wooden seat that ran round the inside of the summer house. Now what was she going to do? It was ages until lunch and she was bored already.

Arabella looked out of the summer house window across the gardens. In the distance she saw the sturdy timber fence that marked the east boundary of her family's property. She could see the outline of a five bar gate that she knew opened into a wood. The village was less than half a mile further on. Arabella had never walked down to the village on her own and she found herself wondering what it would be like. 'Only common, poor people walk anywhere,' said her mother and Arabella believed her.

As Arabella sat looking at the gate she had an idea. 'I know, I'll run away! I'll run away through that gate into those woods, then they'll be sorry. They'll soon wish they had never suggested school.' She stood up and in determined fashion strode out of the summer house and across the gardens heading towards the trees.

The woods wasn't a very accurate term for the little copse that stood just on the other side of Arabella's fence. Many years before, it had been part of a great forest that stretched across the countryside but over the years this had been gradually cut away to make room for the village as it grew. Now there was little more than three or four rows of trees with thin stubbly undergrowth. In spite of this as Arabella came nearer to it she began to feel afraid. Her imagination caused the trees to grow huge and forbidding and she tried hard to remember if Miss Marshall had ever taught her about whether there

Who is hiding in the shadows?
If you would like to find out what happens next,
this book is available now from your local
Christian bookshop..

Save Sam

by Alistair Brown

Rescuing Sam, an abandoned puppy, gave Helen hope that she might at last have a dog of her own. But Sam is put in kennels and Helen discovers he'll die in a week unless she can buy him back. With no money, saving Sam is impossible. Yet Helen knows he's meant to live.

The days tick away and Helen feels desperate. Then a wild storm brings a tree crashing to the ground, and Helen faces an even greater tragedy than the death of a puppy.

Meeting serious problems with only faith and prayer becomes very real for Helen.

ISBN 1-85792-021-X

When the rain came

by Eleanor Watkins

'All his hopes of finding a family had once again been snatched away...Now the dream was shattered just like so many other of his dreams.'

Will anyone ever give Michael the chance to be part of a real family, the one thing which he really longs for? Just as he thinks this is the only storm he has to face, a camping holiday turns out to cause problems which leaves him fighting for his life!

ISBN 1-85792-210-7

Escape to Hong Kong

by Audrey Constant

When Trang arrives in Hong Kong with his sister Mimi and friend Banh, the worst seems over. After a hazardous journey by boat from Vietnam, they are determined to start life afresh. But things don't work out as planned. Mimi, sick from the trials at sea, is taken to hospital, then disappears. Trang in his search for her is drawn into a world of drug smuggling and Triads. All seems lost until he makes a friend.

ISBN 1-85792-063-5

A Voice In The Dark
Richard Wurmbrand

by Catherine Mackenzie

'Where am I? What are you doing? Where are you taking me?' Richard's voice cracked under the strain. His heart was pounding so hard he could hardly breathe. Gasping for air he realized - this was the nightmare! Thoughts came so quickly he could hardly make sense of anything.

'I must keep control,' he said out loud. An evil chuckle broke out from beside him. 'You are no longer in control. We are your worst nightmare!'...

When Richard Wurmbrand is arrested, imprisoned and tortured, he finds himself in utter darkness. Yet the people who put him there discover that their prisoner has a light which can still be seen in the dark - the love of God. This incredible story of one man's faith, despite horrific persecution, is unforgettable and will be an inspiration to all who read it.

ISBN 1-85792-298-0

From Wales to Westminster
Martyn Lloyd-Jones

by his grand-son
Christopher Catherwood

'Fire! Fire!' - A woman shouted frantically. However, as the villagers desperately organised fire fighting equipment the Lloyd-Jones family slept. They were blissfully ignorant that their family home and livelihood was just about to go up in smoke. Martyn, aged ten, was snug in his bed, but his life was in danger.

What happened to Martyn? Who rescued him? How did the fire affect him and his family? And why is somebody writing a book about Martyn in the first place? In this book Christopher Catherwood, Martyn's grandson, tells you about the amazing life of his grandfather, Dr. Martyn Lloyd Jones. Find out about the young boy who trained to be a doctor at just sixteen years old. Meet the young man who was destined to become the Queen's surgeon and find out why he gave it all up to work for God. Read about Martyn Lloyd-Jones. He was enthusiastic and on fire for God. You will be, too, by the end of this book!

ISBN 1-85792-349-9

The Watch-maker's Daughter
Corrie Ten Boom

by Jean Watson

If you like stories of adventure, courage and faith - then here's one you won't forget. Corrie loved to help others, especially handicapped children. But her happy lifestyle in Holland is shattered when she is sent to a Nazi concentration camp. She suffered hardship and punishment but experienced God's love and help in unbearable situations.

Her amazing story has been told worldwide and has inspired many people. Discover about one of the most outstanding Christian women of the 20th century.

ISBN 1-85792-116-X

The Storyteller - C.S. Lewis

by Derick Bingham

C.S.Lewis loved to write stories even as a small child. He grew up to face grief when his mother died, fear when he fought in the First World War and finally love when he realised that God was a God of love and that his son Jesus Christ was the answer to his heart ache.

C.S.Lewis brought this newly discovered joy and wonder into his writings and became known world-wide for his amazing Narnia stories.

Read all about this fascinating man. Find out why his friends called him Jack and not his real name. Find out what C.S.Lewis was really like and discover how one of the greatest writers and academics of the twentieth century turned from atheism to God.

"A good introduction to my stepfather
C. S. Lewis"
Douglas Gresham

ISBN 1-85792-423-1

An Adventure Begins
Hudson Taylor

by Catherine Mackenzie

Hudson Taylor is well-known today as one of the first missionaries to go to China but he wasn't always a missionary. How did he become one then? What was his life like before China? In this book you will meet the Hudson Taylor who lived in Yorkshire as a young boy, fell desperately in love with his sister's music teacher and who struggled to gain independance as a teenager. You will also travel with Hudson to the far east as he obeys God's call to preach the gospel to the Chinese people.

Witness the excitement as he and his sister visit London for the first time, sympathise with the heart-ache as Hudson leaves his family behind to go to China and experience the frustration as his sisters wait for his letters home.

Do you want to know more? Then read this book and let the adventure begin.

ISBN 1-85792-423-1

Look out for
the next in our

TRAIL BLAZERS

series:

George Müller

The children's
champion

written by

Irene Howat

If you like stories of adventure and intrigue, you will love these classic adventures in our Classic Fiction range. These are stories from the dim and distant past but which are just as exciting and relevant as if they were taking place today.

Look out for more titles from this series in the future.

Classic

Fiction

Christie's Old Organ

By O F Walton

Christie knows what it is like to be homeless and on the streets - that's why he is overjoyed to be given a roof over his head by Old Treffy, the Organ Grinder. But Treffy is old and sick and Christie is worried about him. All that Treffy wants is to have peace in his heart and a home of his own. That is what Christie wants too. Christie hears about how Heaven is like Home Sweet Home. Everytime he plays it on Treffy's barrel organ he wonders if he and Treffy can find their way to God's special home. Find out how God uses Christie and the old Barrel organ and lots of friends along the way to bring Treffy and Christie to their own Home Sweet Home.

ISBN: 1-85792-523-8

Classic Fiction

A Peep Behind The Scenes

By O F Walton

Rosalie and her mother are tired of living a life with no home, no security and precious little hope. But Rosalie's father runs a travelling theatre company and the whole family is forced to travel from one town to the next year in year out. Rosalie's father has no objections but Rosalie's mother remembers a better life, before she was married when she had parents who loved her and a sister to play with. Through her memories Rosalie is introduced to the family she never knew she had. Rosalie and her mother are also introduced to somebody else - The Good Shepherd. They hear for the first time about the God who loves them and wants to rescue them and take them to his own home in Heaven. Rosalie rejoices to hear about a real home in Heaven that is waiting for her but will she finally find this other home that she has heard about - or is it too late? Will God help her find her family as he helped her find him? Of course he will!

ISBN 1-85792 -524-6

Classic

Fiction

The Basket of Flowers

By Christoph Von Schmid

Mary grows up sheltered and secure in a beautiful cottage with a loving father. She learns lessons about humility, purity and forgiveness under her father's watchful gaze. However, it doesn't last. Even though she loves God and obeys him this does not protect her ultimately from the envy and hatred of others. Mary is given a generous gift of a new dress from her friend Amelia, the daughter of the local landowner. This incites envy from Juliette, Amelia's maid who had wanted the dress for herself. When Amelia's mother's ring goes missing Juliette decides to pass the blame onto Mary. Both Mary and her father are imprisoned for the crime and eventually exciled from their home. Mary learns to trust in God completely as difficulty follows after difficulty. Even when she doubts if she will ever clear her name she turns back to God who is a constant source of comfort to her. Who did steal the ring in the end? That is the final unexpected twist in the tale which makes this book a really good read.

ISBN 1-85792 -525-4

CHRISTIAN FOCUS

Good books with the real message of hope!

Christian Focus Publications publishes biblically-accurate books for adults and children.

If you are looking for quality bible teaching for children then we have a wide and excellent range of bible story books - from board books to teenage fiction, we have it covered.

You can also try our new Bible teaching Syllabus for 3-9 year olds and teaching materials for pre-school children.

These children's books are bright, fun and full of biblical truth, an ideal way to help children discover Jesus Christ for themselves. Our aim is to help children find out about God and get them enthusiastic about reading the Bible, now and later in their life.

**Find us at our web page:
www.christianfocus.com**